STORIES OF PLACE

///zinc.level.blindfold

An Anthology

Edited by
Niamh McAnally

With stories by
Emile Cassen, Lily Devalle, Sandy Foster, Billy Green,
Catherine Johnstone, Conor McAnally,
Niamh McAnally, Nina Smith, Ben Tufnell

Black Rose Writing | Texas

The author grants the final approval for this literary material.

First printing

This is a work of fiction. Names, characters, businesses, places, events, and incidents are either the products of the author's imagination or used in a fictitious manner. Any resemblance to actual persons, living or dead, or actual events is purely coincidental.

ISBN: 978-1-68513-588-1
PUBLISHED BY BLACK ROSE WRITING
www.blackrosewriting.com

Printed in the United States of America
Suggested Retail Price (SRP) $19.95

Stories of Place is printed in Book Antiqua

*As a planet-friendly publisher, Black Rose Writing does its best to eliminate unnecessary waste to reduce paper usage and energy costs, while never compromising the reading experience. As a result, the final word count vs. page count may not meet common expectations.

Praise for *Stories of Place*

"A varied and eclectic collection, showcasing new writers of promise. There are voices here I hope we'll be hearing more from."
–Mick Herron, author, CWA Steel and Gold Dagger winner, creator of *Slow Horses*

"I loved these short, fantastic plunges into such vivid worlds."
–Ross Armstrong, author of *Sunday Times* best seller *The Watcher*

"A wonderful undertaking - a moving collection run through with humanity and humour, in turns moving and challenging, bringing a wide range of characters (and writers) together into a complementary and satisfying whole."
–Nick Clark Windo, author of *The Feed*

"*Stories of Place: zinc.level.blindfold* is a kaleidoscope of narratives where each story is a universe unto itself, weaving together a tapestry of emotions, genres, and perspectives. Embark on a journey through the human experience with exquisitely crafted prose that spans from fantastical whimsy to haunting introspection, encouraging readers to ponder the intricate complexities of life."
–Gayle Brown, award-winning author of *A Deadly Game*

"An anthology of short stories should bring to the reader a kaleidoscope of genres, techniques, emotions and challenges: *Stories of Place* delivers in every department. Decorated with works that surprise and delight the audience, while giving us pause to reflect and equate the emotions therein to our own lives. Niamh McAnally has pulled together an exquisite assortment of tales that keep us turning to the next instalment, eager to be carried away with their words again and again. Recommended."
–J.A. Marley, author of the *Danny Felix* series

"*Stories of Place* offers a fascinating collection of eighteen short stories by nine authors. Each story offering a jolt of caffeine strained through a prism of contrasting experiences of the human condition. This collection of stories is both relatable and unforgettable!"
–Jay Jay French, Twisted Sister

"These eighteen short stories by a group of highly talented writers span the globe: geographical locations include Ireland, Tokyo, New York and London. However, what makes them collectively so compelling is the way they both head into a rich landscape of the past - whether a tour of duty in Iraq or a derelict house - and an equally thoughtful and compelling internal world. With memory clinics, taekwondo competitions and corporate culture taken to extremes, contemporary 21st century life also feels fully mapped in these tales."
–Sarah Turner, travel writer, *Forbes Online* and *The Sunday Times*

"Extraordinary events unfold in these distinctive, plangent tales - of chronic amnesia and a parasitical stranger; of a childhood curdled by a dark discovery; of a woman overcoming trauma through martial arts. Stories of loneliness, triumph and acceptance. Whether haunted or healed by their locations, each writer uses place as a springboard for a powerful imaginative leap."
–Sam Kenyon, author of *I am not Raymond Wallace* and playwright of *Miss Littlewood*

"A tender homage to human experiences and the places they are anchored to. Bewildering, uplifting, heartbreaking, relatable or enlightening, each story is crafted with palpable skill and a distinct authorial voice that will linger long after the final line."
–Anne Freeman, award-winning author

"These diverse characters come alive under the expertise of these great writers. The tales will find their way to the heart and take up residence."
–Max (Maxi) McCoubrey, singer, songwriter and TV presenter

"Whenever I open any anthology, I expect some pieces to resonate more than others. But what sets *Stories of Place* apart is the quality of the work. Under the deft hand of curator and contributing writer Niamh McAnally, each story is honed to a fine point. Some break the surface of the skin; others cut right to the heart. Stephen King said, 'Fiction is the truth inside the lie,' and that's what you'll find here — glaring truth. The stories comprising this book are more than compelling vignettes; they are corridors into the abyss of each writer's soul. Sometimes you'll discover unexpected light there, sometimes darkness. But always, *always* you will find honesty in this unique collection of tales well told."
–Bob Massey, award-winning journalist and editor

"What an incredible collection of short stories filled with such vivid characters that take us deep into the fragility of the human condition. Entertaining, thrilling and absolutely thought-provoking, these stories collectively weave a sweeping thematic journey of failure and redemption, love and loss. This is a read that will stay with you long after you turn the final page. I cannot recommend it enough."
–John Wynn, director, *The Rising Hawk*

"These are masterfully crafted stories that invite us to intimately encounter the raw urgency of our emotions and drives. They allow the reader to encounter nuance and the shadowy subtleties of 21st century life, leaving space for passion and uncertainty."
–Dr Dennis Tirch, author, psychologist, Center for Compassion Focused Therapy, New York

"A fantastic collection, as well as a testament to the importance of discovering and sustaining a writing community."
–Jack Hadley, Senior Courses Manager, Curtis Brown Creative

In loving memory of
Wendy Williams

To Mick,

Thanks for your support
& wisdom, which keeps me
keep on keeping on.

Cheers,

Billy.

STORIES
OF PLACE

Contents

Introduction

On a sunny June day in Ipswich, UK, this group of writers: Emile Cassen, Lily Devalle, Sandy Foster, Billy Green, Cathy Johnstone, Conor McAnally, Nina Smith, Ben Tufnell and myself, Niamh McAnally, hugged for the very first time. We'd come from Australia, America, Ireland and all over England. While we'd never met in person before, over the previous three years we'd shared more about ourselves with each other than perhaps with members of our own families. We'd laid bare our souls and felt united by a need to tell our stories and create meaning through the written word. Originally, we were a group of ten. Missing from our gathering that summer's day was an author known for her children's books, Wendy Williams, who sadly passed away the same week.

Our journey began in 2020. We each had a first draft of a manuscript and the desire to make it better. Curtis Brown Creative's six-week online writing course, Edit and Pitch Your Novel, provided that opportunity. One of the weekly assignments was to post our work on a forum for peer review. A daunting undertaking. Not only did this entail exposing one's early drafts to strangers, it also required learning how to provide feedback in a positive manner. One end of the see-saw offered excessive praise, the other, criticism rather than constructive commentary. Finding the balance was challenging. I believed that fellow students might find that sweet spot by being invested in each other's success. I invited my classmates to meet via Zoom and get to know the person behind the words. What transpired was a desire to critique with care. Words became polished by input from others, sentences developed syntax from valuable suggestions. Comments like 'I'm looking forward to reading more of your work,' were heartfelt. By the end of the course, there was a collective energy: a tribe was forming and I didn't want to let the momentum die. And so this international writer's group was born.

Since then, we've met online every month. We've created a safe space where we feel free from fear of failure and plagiarism. We've held each other accountable to our writing goals. Like many professions in the creative arts, the author's path to publication is plagued with rejection. Our strength comes from the sum of the group and the commitment to lift each other out of those moments of self-doubt. We celebrate each other's successes, both large and small, as if they were our own, and now, between us, we've had our work long- and shortlisted in various competitions, attained literary awards, and been published by mainstream and small presses.

We are a diverse group of writers. Our storytelling crosses many genres, from fast-paced thrillers to quiet family sagas, from literary musings to tender memoirs and from tales of adventure to LGBTQ+ and coming-of-age narratives. And so it was, at our first writers' retreat in 2023, we discussed the idea of bringing some of those stories together. But how would we marry our eclectic styles to compose an anthology with a central theme? It was Emile Cassen who came up with the suggestion of tying our stories together via ///what3words. At the time, not all of us were familiar with this geocode system. Emile explained the concept: An algorithm has divided the surface of Earth into three-metre by three-metre squares – 57 trillion of them – and gives each a unique three-word address.

The idea came about when event organizers, Chris Sheldrick and Mohan Ganesalingham, frequently struggled to get bands and their equipment to precise locations of concert venues. Having teamed with linguist Jack Waley-Cohen and tech entrepreneur Michael Dent, the four designed and created the app in 2013. With support from Intel, Mercedes, Ikea, ITV and many car companies, it has gone on to assist businesses, organisations and even national administrations across the world. For instance, countries where named streets are few, like the Kingdom of Tonga, Mongolia, St Maarten and Côte d'Ivoire, have adopted ///what3words addresses for their postal deliveries. Many emergency services have used the system to find kayakers in trouble at sea, disoriented mountaineers off the grid, and injured hillwalkers far from trails. The three-word address for the exact three-square metre spot on which you stand is much simpler to convey than coordinates of longitude and latitude.

Embracing the concept for this anthology, we decided to title each story with one of the three-word addresses in which it was set. As the reader, you can look up the title and identify the location before you begin, or glean the general area from the context and then verify your findings afterwards. If you check out the title of this collection: ///zinc.level.blindfold, you'll find the patio where we were sitting when we brainstormed the idea for this collaborative work.

Whether you are reading these stories in order, by author, or by dipping in and out, have fun! And if you would like to spread the word, we invite you to add a photo of this book on your social media and mention the ///what3words location in which you read it.

–Niamh McAnally

///corrode.ends.arriving
by Sandy Foster

They arrived on the Sunday, just after I'd finished a late lunch, the unwashed pots and pans still stacked by the sink. When I answered the door, I found a neat person standing on the doorstep: hair parted at the side, clothes ironed, shoes polished. I even noticed their hands, nails clipped and clean. Respectable. The sort of person one could happily share a table with at a restaurant. A person you could safely loan money to. And at their feet, as if they'd been standing long enough on my doorstep to tire of holding onto it, was a brown leather suitcase, covered in stickers of various places visited: Milan, New York, Hawaii. Like they'd walked right out of an old black and white film about train stations and strangers, unrequited love and strained goodbyes. They gave me a look of such familiarity, such unbound pleasure, a smile glued across their face, ears flexing with the effort, that I felt that old panic rising up and the realisation that I must know this person, and know them pretty well for them to be standing here, at the front of my house, arms spread wide in greeting.

This happens to me a lot. I'm walking down the street and someone will call my name, rush through the traffic to ask how I am, if things are busy at work, how my holiday was. And I will not know them. Face blindness, they call it. An inability to immediately recognise someone, even if you've known that person for ten years, even if that person is your own mother. As a child, people would chalk it up as shyness or an inability to stand still long enough to allow for pleasantries. A propensity toward thoughtfulness and solitude, perhaps. Children have greater things occupying them than social etiquette. Monsters to fight and spaceships to fly. But the older one gets, the less endearing, the less excusable it becomes.

The first few times it happened to me as an adult I'd look blank, confess I had no idea who I was speaking to, that I was certain we'd never met. But I quickly learnt to disguise my uneasy amnesia. After you've upset your old schoolteacher or third cousin once removed, you realise that little lies make for less trouble. Of late, I tend to listen and nod and agree until some vague memory pops up from nowhere. *Ah yes, it's the distressed lady from the bakery.* Then a connection might jump into my head or an event, a shared experience and I can ask, *did you ever find your dog? How were the cinnamon buns? Remind me, what was your name again?* And then I will truly engage, with the shape of the eyes, the way the cupid's bow dips and glides, the tiny hairs across the upper lip. I will burn the image of them into my mind so that it never, ever happens again.

Sometimes, rarely I suppose, but it does happen, sometimes no memory will come to me at all. I will listen and nod and agree, the whole time having absolutely no idea who I am speaking to. I'm sure they must see it on my face, the blankness in my eyes, the rising redness in my cheeks. It's a relief when they finally walk away and leave me to my private confusion, but it's also terribly, terribly humiliating, to be so useless in this way. This affliction isn't borne out of disinterest or arrogance. I have many friends; I am a social creature. It's just my little weakness. Some people can't recall phone numbers, others forget where they left their keys. I can't remember faces.

So, when this person arrived on that otherwise quiet afternoon, interrupted by only the gentle purr of distant lawn mowers, I was unsurprised to find myself utterly flummoxed by the presence of what felt like a total stranger. They hugged me and held my face as if it might at any minute roll from my neck. They asked me how I'd been, saying *how good it is to see you, how bright and happy you look since last time*. I thought, last time, when was *last time*? What had happened *last time* that made me dull and flat? They must have noticed the flicker of doubt that meandered across my face because they asked, *you knew to expect me didn't you, you didn't forget?* The awkwardness had me immediately apologising, explaining, *of course not, no, come in, come in*, so that moments later, the face I did not recognise was standing in my hallway, taking off their jacket, throwing down their case next to my orderly lined-up shoes. I reassured myself there was nothing to fret about, that it would come to me any moment now, something in the way they laughed or pulled off their scarf. Something about the way they touched my arm or walked toward my kitchen with the familiarity of an old friend would trigger a memory. Then I would be able to relax and join in with the conversation. Allow myself to be present.

I filled the kettle and fetched two cups, but even there I was set with a problem. Did they even drink tea, did I know them too well to ask? I was swiftly saved from the dilemma when they efficiently took over as if it were in fact their home, locating the teabags and sugar, pouring the milk into the small porcelain jug.

Once the tea was prepared and a little plate of custard creams laid out on the tray, I took us into the lounge where we sat. Thankfully, the person mostly talked at me, of trips away to the seaside and how their mother's getting on in the home, just the usual chat one might have with a close acquaintance. Every so often they stood; wandered around the room, fingered the bookshelves, peered at the pictures on the walls. They commented on the small pink lamp on the side table and asked if it were new. When they excused themselves to use the bathroom, I looked at my watch. Ten past ten. I had spent over six hours with them and not a single clue had revealed itself. The time was a reassurance, I thought, for they would surely go soon, and then I could sit in the dark and wrack my brains, or at least forget about them forever. I would be left with nothing but the buzzing of the fridge and my own cringing. When they returned, they looked at their watch and I thought, this is it, the moment I can be left in peace. *Gosh, its late,* they said. *I don't know about you, but I'm usually in bed by half nine. I hope you don't think me rude –* Not at all, I protested, *of course of course, thank you for coming.* We stood in the thickness of a short silence, waiting for one of us to move. *So, where am I sleeping?* they asked.

I lay awake most of the night. The strange face was asleep on my fold-out bed in the lounge. I tried to comb through the details, the laugh exploding out of them in puffs like a car trying to start, the way they gesticulated when animated, the crepe folds of their neck. I recalled the things they spoke of, the cans of tuna ordered in bulk by mistake, the cancer treatment endured the year before, the budgerigar that was violently attacked by the cat. Surely one of those details should pop through the unfamiliarity of their face and reveal itself in sharp relief? When I eventually fell asleep, the light was already beginning to seep through the curtains and I dreamt of my teeth falling out.

I awoke suddenly as if my sleep had been shallow, just below the surface of consciousness, a permanent awareness of the stranger breathing in the room below me. It was just before nine. I usually rise much earlier, and was mortified that I'd left someone to potter alone downstairs in my home. I hoped for a moment it had just been a dream, but the banging of cupboards and clinking of cups below was enough for me to know the strange face was still there.

I arrived downstairs to find them in the kitchen, munching through a slice of toast. They'd made a pot of coffee and were reading the local newspaper, which always comes on a Monday. *Good afternoon sleepy head,* they said with a smirk, *hope you don't mind,* indicating the crumpled paper, stained with buttery fingers. I love the local news. The stories of lost cats and bake sales, the photos of the boules team and the village green maypole. Something about the quiet, mundanity of its contents soothes me. Monday mornings are my favourite day of the week for this, opening the crisp sheets, reading it cover to cover. *Not at all,* I said, *of course of course. Help yourself, what's mine is yours.* The relief I felt that this strange face would soon be gone made me hospitality personified. *Any plans today?* I asked, in a way that felt casual, no rush, do as you please and I shall tiptoe around you. *I thought we could go for a walk,* they replied. *You could show me the area.* A stone dropped into my stomach.

While they ate their breakfast and perused the paper, I set about tidying away the sofa bed. I have always found it a pleasing contraption, the way it folds in on itself and snaps back into place when you lift the handle, neatly tucking within like a sleeping animal, cushions covering it as if it were never there. I folded the spare duvet and placed the pillows on top, ready to be returned to the airing cupboard. I retreated upstairs to shower and used the opportunity of the water to wash me clean of any anxiety. The identity of the strange face would surely come to me, any moment now. The water ran down my neck in little rivulets, pooling at my feet. Before long, I was standing in several inches of water and when I looked down, I saw the plug hole was blocked by a mass of black hair. A little creature burrowed at my feet. Not my hair.

We spent the day walking through the village. I pointed out the various houses that held some kind of history, the cottage crumbling around the couple whose daughter died in an accident; the driveway with the rusted caravan, belonging to the man with the gambling addiction; the prize-winning garden with the pogonias and the gnomes and the yapping shih tzu. We walked through the cemetery where I pointed out my father's grave, meticulously weeded, flowers blooming in little pots. They made empathetic noises and I couldn't work out if they knew my father or not. I enjoyed the strange face's company, in spite of the creeping nag at my insides, the knowledge that I had absolutely no idea who they were. They were charming, warm in a way I'd not felt in a while. I was reminded every so often of their anonymity, by a mention of their own lives, or a leading question about my past. But mostly, it was easy to forget they were a stranger to me. Easy to forget who I was in this context. We shared an afternoon tea in the café near the post office and fed the ducks at the pond, watching the pieces of bread spin in the dark water. I showed them every inch of my little village, so that by the time we returned to the house, it was late afternoon and the sun was beginning to retreat behind the garden shed. The strange face made no sign of leaving, so I offered them dinner and they sat and watched me cook. When I opened the cupboard that should house the pasta, I found the contents had completely changed. It was no longer stacked with canned beans and soup, packets of pasta and rice, but baking goods. I stood for a moment in confusion, door open, fingers still clasped around the handle. *I hope you don't mind. I thought it was silly having all your baking goods crammed into the drawer. And having to reach up like that, every time you need to make dinner for yourself. You'll do your back in.* I pulled open the drawer, and there were all the things that should have been in the cupboard. They looked neat, orderly, as if they'd always been there. The cans sat perfectly flush with the top of the drawer and I wondered why I'd never thought of that. A pang of irritation was quickly suppressed. It's difficult to be angry when someone was only trying to help, when someone seemed to instinctively see the answers to all the little inconveniences you've learnt to live with. As I closed the door, I felt a small twinge in my lower back, a pain I now recalled had been there for an eternity.

After dinner, I washed up and the strange face disappeared into the lounge, presumably to pack their things and be on their way. I looked out the kitchen window at a fox as it stalked across my lawn. It momentarily glanced directly at me, the threat of a challenge in its eyes. It dipped its long nose to the ground in a bow or in preparation to pounce, I'm not sure which, the shoulders visibly flexing, and then it was gone in an instant, as if chasing some invisible force. When I finished, I moved into the lounge, still drying my hands on a tea towel. The strange face had unfolded the bed, replaced the duvet and pillow, and stood in their pyjamas, brushing their hair. I fell asleep quickly this time, but dreamt vividly and several times I sat up suddenly, in a cold sweat.

The next day, my alarm woke me early so I might get myself ready for work and politely usher the stranger out the door. But when I got downstairs, the stranger looked as though they'd been up for hours already, or perhaps they hadn't slept at all, like some nocturnal creature. They were quietly reading one of my books on the sofa, a book I was a third of the way through already, the bed having retreated for the day. They had made themselves a pot of tea, a half-eaten digestive resting on the saucer. I was annoyed that despite the alarm, the need to get to work, the strange face had still beaten me to it, woken earlier, leaving me feeling lazy in my own home. I explained that I must work today, but they assured me *that's fine, leave me a key and I can pootle about, no problem at all.* I smiled sweetly, apologised for not being around despite the roaring in my gut, told them to make themselves at home, help themselves to anything they needed. And I ushered myself out of the house.

I spent the day at work only half there. I stared at the computer screen willing myself to focus but the words seem to shudder and vibrate. Away from them, I couldn't picture the stranger, couldn't conjure up the shape of their nose or colour of their eyes, despite the twenty-four hours spent with them already. Their face was a blur, a smudge, a featureless thumb. When colleagues asked me how I was, what I did with my weekend, I found myself smiling, nodding, lying. *Oh, a quiet one*, I said, *nothing unusual*. I'm confused by my own self-imposed deception. I can only assume it was shame that prevented me telling anyone I had a stranger sleeping in my lounge. I stayed later than usual, and it was only the sudden switching off of automatic lights and the sound of the hoover being driven across the tiled carpet flooring that alerted me to the time.

On the drive home I convinced myself that I would return to a note from the stranger, an apology for leaving without a goodbye and a name signed at the bottom that would finally solve the mystery. But as I pulled onto the driveway, the flickering light of the television through the lounge curtains told me they were still there, growing into the sofa. As I opened the front door, I called out, not wanting to alarm the stranger in my own house by suddenly appearing. *Only me*, I said, as if it might be anyone else. They glanced up as I popped my head into the lounge, gave me a little wave, fully absorbed in whatever it was they were watching. My cat was curled up on their lap and they ran their fingers back and forth through her fur. *There's soup in the pan and bread on the side*, they muttered with barely a look to me. I crept past into the kitchen, as if it were me and not the stranger who was the guest. When I entered the kitchen, I saw the dining table had changed angle, so the length of it sat parallel with the French doors. It gave a better view of the garden like that. I ate the soup leaning against the sink.

I worked the rest of the week, each morning expecting the stranger to leave, each evening returning to find them still there, wiping down my surfaces, eating my food, moving pieces of furniture. On Thursday night, I arrived home to find the lounge empty, but with the bed made up, a pair of my pyjamas neatly folded on the pillow. The stranger appeared in the doorway behind me, framed like a surrealist painting. *I hope you don't mind,* they said, *I'm having such difficulty sleeping and after last time you said I only had to say.* I spent the night on the sofa bed, the springs sagging beneath me.

When Sunday arrives once more, I feel a wave of panic at the fact an entire week has passed, followed by relief that surely now the stranger will leave. The shame of my inability to remember them has kept me from asking them to go and my desire to be polite has impressed upon them a reason to stay. So today, a full week since their arrival, will be the day I ask them to leave. I can do this, I tell myself. I dance around the subject for most of the morning, asking them what their plans are, if they need anything else, how they got here, but something in the strange face has changed. They are colder, less inclined to talk. When a grumble in my stomach alerts me that it's lunchtime, I ignore it, in the hope my lack of hospitality will see them off, but nonetheless they make themselves a sandwich. Just before three, I decide to go for a walk. I can't bear to be around the strange face any longer and I get the impression they too have had enough of me. I slowly amble across the playing field, stopping to watch an under-eights five-a-side football match, one child's face dripping with snot and tears. I pass by the church, watch a man arguing with his dog, the vicar talking to someone in the shade of the oak tree. I walk down the many alleyways, past the house with the cat staring out into the cold street and the abandoned bungalow with the upturned wheelbarrow.

By the time I make it back to the house, it's getting dark and the wind has picked up. I stand on the doorstep, fumbling for my keys. The lounge curtains are closed and no light shines through, but when I look up, I see the bedroom is occupied, a shadow passing by the window. When I try to put my key in the lock, it seems to have grown extra teeth as metal hits metal. I squint my eyes, turn the key over, try again. There are only three possibilities on the keyring: one for the front door, one for the shed where I keep my bike and the other for work. I try all three, even though I know without a doubt which one is meant for the front door. None of them fit. I look down at the bundle of keys in my hand. Perhaps none of these are for this door. Perhaps this door is not mine at all. Because if it were mine, why would I be standing out here in the cold?

I look up at the house. I could have sworn this was my house once, the door, the mat, the driveway. It all feels so familiar. But if it was mine then I'd be inside it, wouldn't I? I look back up at the bedroom. The shadow walks up to the window and draws the curtains across. Then the lights go out. I walk back down the driveway. I no longer know where I am. Who I am. It all feels so familiar and yet so strange, so distant. I am sure I lived here once.

Or somewhere like this.

///brave.acted.fall
by Niamh McAnally

Doctor Carol had fifteen minutes to spare before her next patient. The herb supplements she'd recently swallowed to ease her headache seemed to be mocking her. Despite her profession as a doctor of Chinese medicine, she was tempted to embrace western pharmacology and take a couple of paracetemols. Anything to silence the drummer who had taken up residency in her temporal lobe. But she picked up her phone instead and clicked on the green owl. The Duolingo icon revealed today's language lesson.

As soon as Ireland had offered to harbour the women, children, and the wounded fleeing from the war in Ukraine, Doctor Carol had tried to learn a few words of their mother tongue. For many, the Cyrillic alphabet was difficult to grasp but Carol had flirted with Mandarin during her studies in China. She'd always found it easy to absorb a language in the country where it was spoken, but to learn Ukrainian she had to settle for an online course. She'd chosen Duolingo, and used the free service, despite the annoying ads. Today's first new word sounded like *voy-batch-te*. English translation: sorry. '*Voy-batch-te*' she repeated. *Ping*. The owl approved of her pronunciation. But not for long. Carol was unfocused. Each mistake cost her one of the five hearts the app allocated. When she lost the final one, the lesson halted. The owl asked if she would like to upgrade to the paid service so she could continue. No, she would not. But the damn bird asked every day. Even though she didn't want to break her 312-day streak of learning, she knew she could wait it out until the bird refilled those hearts.

'*Voy-batch-te,*' she repeated to herself as she put the phone down. 'Sorry.' God, was she ever sorry. If only she could begin yesterday again. She was a healer and when she couldn't heal, she hurt. That hurt had turned inward and become anger, an anger she had soothed with wine. This morning's headache was accentuated by the usual bitterness. Why had her husband hidden the truth all those years ago?

Her vocation as an acupuncturist had begun in 1983 when she was twelve years old. Her mam had taken her and her brother to Spain – a holiday to distract them from the cavernous hole left by her father's unexpected death. It was a sunny November day, a paradox for a child who'd never been out of Ireland before. The three of them had been riding donkeys, or *burros* as the nice man had called them, on a trail near Torremolinos. When her brother poked her donkey with a stick, the animal took off, galloping, dust billowing from its hooves. It was probably only a trot, but compared to its previous sedentary plod, it felt like galloping to Carol. She clung to the stubby hair on its neck, her heart matching his pounding hooves. The guide whistled, and the donkey came to an abrupt stop. Young Carol somersaulted off its back, and was stabbed by an enormous cactus plant on her way to the ground. She heard her mother scream.

'Oh my God, baby, oh my God!'

Then she felt someone pulling her up. Large needles protruded from Carol's palms and inner forearms.

'I'm OK, Mam. I'm OK.'

And strangely, she was. Instead of pain, Carol could feel a smile turning her lips upwards. She didn't understand why, but just knew she felt better than she had since her daddy died. Weeks later, it was her very wise pen-pal in California, the daughter of an acupuncturist, who told her about Chinese medicine, and about energy pathways in the body. It was possible that the needles had embedded themselves along one of the meridians, which helped with processing grief. Carol had never heard of meridians or acupoints, but whatever they were she wanted to learn more. She wanted to be able to make her family feel this calmness too. So began her journey into understanding the healing powers of acupuncture, and a career that would bring her international recognition for her work with pregnant women whose bodies went into labour too soon.

The first time she'd helped an expectant mother suppress premature contractions was a venture into new healing territory. The baby had been resting low in the woman's belly, but halfway through the treatment, both Carol and the mother experienced the shift. The baby moved upwards. After she'd helped four more women arrest early labour, she became committed to researching how acupuncture might save tiny lives. Each case was different, but she developed a strategy to rebalance the qi in the patient's body while applying acupressure to a point on the scalp. Her success rate was so remarkable that her findings were published in The Journal of Chinese Medicine. From then on, she was affectionately known as The Baby Whisperer.

But yesterday she couldn't save an unborn from being born too soon. Even though the woman had been forty-two, and the pregnancy had been considered high risk, Carol berated herself for not being able to do more. It had been the woman's last chance at motherhood and Carol felt her loss as if it was her own.

She shook herself, tried to shut out the spinning thoughts. She checked her watch. Ten o'clock. Time to bring Natalia in. At least she wasn't 'with child'. Carol opened the door to the waiting room and was surprised to see that her patient was accompanied by a young man. He was pale and scrawny; his left arm hung in a sling.

'Hello, Doctor,' Natalia said in her soft Ukrainian accent.

'Hello, love. And who's this with you, today?'

'This is Pavlik. He is from small village.' Natalia's English had improved immensely since she'd arrived in Dublin a year ago, along with hundreds of other refugees. Maybe the owl gave her more than five hearts. Natalia deserved them though. It took courage to raise two teenage children in a foreign country while her husband and eldest son remained behind to fight.

'Hello Pavlik,' Carol said, offering the young fella her hand. 'Lovely to meet you.' He didn't shake it but glanced at Natalia, then looked down.

Natalia said: 'Pavlik bring me news from home.'

'Good news, I hope?'

'No.'

'Oh.'

'My son is dead.'

'Oh, Natalia, I'm so sorry.'

'Pavlik come to tell me, himself.'

Carol put an arm around Natalia's shoulder. 'Come on in, love, let's get you on the table.'

'No, not me. I give my appointment to Pavlik. He has the sadness inside him,' she said, pointing at his chest.

'Oh. Did he know your son?'

'In the war, yes.'

Carol looked at the waif of a young man, his forehead was crumpled, etched in a frown, his eyes, dark.

'Please, Doctor, he needs your help.'

'Of course. But let me take care of you afterwards.'

'Thank you,' said Natalia.

Carol led Pavlik into the treatment room. He was cautious, kept looking at the door.

'Would you like to lie on the table?'

He shrugged. She mimed lying down. He pointed at his boots. She indicated it was OK to take them off. Since his injured arm would make it difficult for him to undo his laces, Carol moved to help him. He jumped backwards.

'It's OK, you're OK,' she tried to reassure him. But Pavlik remained wary. Carol sat down and waited, hoping to gain his trust. He watched her. She nodded at his boots; he nodded towards the door. Understanding him, she invited Natalia to come in and translate.

'Can you tell him it's OK to take off his boots.'

Natalia spoke to him in hushed tones. He said something in return.

'He wants me to stay. OK?'

'Sure.'

Natalia helped him lie down, all the time talking softly to him. She untied the laces and removed his boots and socks. He seemed to relax more in her presence.

'Thank you. Why don't you sit here?'

Natalia sat in the small armchair facing the table.

Carol turned the lights down and eased the pan-pipe music up. Pavlik lay still. When she popped in the first few needles, he didn't flinch, but as soon as she placed one on the inside of his forearm, about three fingers from the crease of his wrist, he started to cry. Slow tears at first. Carol had expected it. This acupoint, she now knew as Pericardium 6, was one she used often for emotional release. But Pavlik's tears became sobs, sobs turned into howls.

'*Izvini*,' he cried out. '*Izvini*.'

It was not a Ukrainian word Carol recognised.

Natalia, too, began to cry. She stood up and went to him, stroked his forehead and whispered in his ear. His sobs began to subside. But still he repeated '*Izvini*.' Softer now. '*Izvini*.'

'What's he saying?'

'He say he is sorry.'

'Sorry?' Carol thought back to her Duolingo lesson from earlier. 'I thought the word for sorry was *Voy-batch-te*. I just learned it today.'

'Yes, it is . . . But . . . He is speaking Russian.'

'Russian? Why?'

Natalia inhaled; her chest expanded. She paused before speaking. It was as if she was trying to make up her mind. 'Pavlik is from Russia.'

'Russia? What? How did he get here?'

'He escape. He come with refugee plane. He come to Dublin to find me.'

Natalia turned back to Pavlik and stroked his wet cheek. 'He come to tell me he is sorry. To tell me . . . to tell me he kill my son.'

Carol's hand flew to her mouth. Her pulse pounded. Her brain couldn't cope with another woman losing a child. And *this mother*, this mother was stroking the face of the person who had killed her boy.

'Natalia! How can you do this? How can you possibly forgive him?'

'I must. I must forgive. I forgive; I feel better.'

'He killed your son!'

'Yes,' said Natalia. 'But look at him, Doctor Carol. He has nineteen years of age. A boy, like my son. They tell him to fight. He fight. He is Russian, but he is victim of this war too, no?'

Carol took three deep breaths to centre herself and carried on treating Pavlik. When she was finished, Natalia slipped Pavlik's feet into his boots, laced them up and helped him off the bed. Gone was his frown; his eyes looked lighter.

'I come tomorrow?' Natalia asked.

'Of course.'

After they left, Carol slumped in the chair and let her own tears escape. She wept for the babies she had not be able to save, for the children she, herself, would never have, for the years she'd blamed herself for her empty womb, for the husband who had denied her motherhood. If only he'd been honest before they got married and told her he could not father a child. She had never forgiven him for that. Yet, here was Natalia, a mother whose grown son would never come home, a mother who knew that to survive the pain she had to make peace with it, to forgive.

Natalia was right: I forgive, I feel better.

It reminded Carol to focus on why she had become an acupuncturist. She wanted to help people heal, and neither judgement nor blame had any place in her practice. The first person she needed to heal, though, was herself. It was time to cast off her resentment towards her husband. Perhaps if she'd had children of her own, she may not have such empathy for expectant mothers desperate to save their unborn. It was time to evaluate her life anew and to be grateful for the blessings she did have. She would begin by focusing on things she was free to do that women raising children were not.

Her phone pinged. The Duolingo icon had a red dot in the corner, a notification that her hearts were now full, and she could continue her lessons.

///limp.shield.glaze
by Lily Devalle

Helmet, check. Shin guards, body armour, check.

Butterflies, check.

Her kit had been carefully packed the night before, but now Stella stares at the disemboweled bag, contents sprawled across her bedroom. She bites a cuticle, taking final inventory.

Bradford wanders over, sits on the uniform she had so meticulously ironed.

'No! Bad boy. *Mooove!*' She rarely yells at her sweet lab.

She slides down the foot of her bed to the floor and sighs. For a moment, her mind clocks this as resignation, a premature defeat.

Give it up, already. Why are you doing this to yourself, your body, again?

But Stella knows why. She scoots forward, slides her phone from her back pocket. There's still time for her meditation. Still time to build a seawall, stop the rising tide of self-doubt.

She rests the phone against crossed legs, hits play. Her mind conjures up the blue and red gym. She visualises how she'll walk into it, how she'll interact in it, how she'll perform in it. The soft voice guiding her is soothing, and she repeats the manifestations out loud.

'I am achieving my dreams. I am attracting success.'

Bradford plops down next to her, his warm body pressing into her side. She strokes his head, refocuses on the mantras.

'I release myself from the past.'

'I am present. I am strong.'

But defence-building is harder that morning. Her foot starts to twitch, then her entire leg. The taste of banana smoothie revisits, its thickness not enough to coat and settle the butterflies.

How could one place bring so much joy yet so much fear at the same time?

Her mind springboards back to the bag. She opens her eyes, catapults up, repacks everything just so.

In the bathroom, she slips on her elbow brace, then carefully wraps Kinesio tape around her ankle, under her foot. Other injuries are too internal, too deep, to wrap.

In the kitchen, she collects her water bottle, her nuts. She throws back a handful of supplements, washes them down with Lucozade. A Ziplock bag of homemade protein bars alongside a note are displayed on the counter – an apology for missing her big day.

She pulls out her phone, opens the flight app. The little plane shows her husband is somewhere over the Atlantic. Her stomach protests his absence for her.

Scrolling to the taxi app, she checks her cab, pre-ordered the night before.

Nerves affect her driving. Public transport affects her nerves.

The app shows a ten-minute delay. Then another ten.

'What the heck is going on?' she says to no one.

The driver calls. Stuck due to the Hackney half-marathon.

Shit.

Desperate times call for the Vespa.

On the street, she frees her girl from lock and chain. No time to wipe off city grime. She awkwardly balances the enormous

Taekwondo bag on the floorboard between her legs. With a wobble, she pulls off.

A few blocks down and there they are, panting with pride. She straddles bike and bag, watching the runners in fascination. For a moment, she imagines climbing off, abandoning her heavy bag, running with them. Running away.

But she'd never disappoint Master. Or herself.

Instead, she waits for a gap in the sea of bodies. She slides off, pushes the scooter with all her strength across Queensland Road. Obstacle cleared!

Stella releases a forceful breath as she pushes through the door of the dojang. There's no turning back now. She charges down the stairs, bag banging awkwardly against her leg. Her frenetic entrance is greeted with a *tisk* by the hotshot kid manning the front desk.

'*Ooooh,* you're late!'

'Umm, thanks. I know.'

She darts past fellow students doing what she had planned: warming up, stretching, rehearsing. The smell of nervous sweat already permeates the blue and red gym.

Alone in the changing room, she sits for a moment, eyes closed, with the fluttering inside. She takes two or three breaths with intent. There's no time for any breathing exercises. Her hand plunges into the big bag. She pulls out her uniform and crumbs fly everywhere like confetti.

What the . . .

The Ziplock. The protein bar has exploded everywhere. Putting on her uniform, she sheds remnants as she shimmies in. She ignores this, focuses on carefully tying her black belt. Unsatisfied with the first knot, she releases it in a huff and tries again.

The booming voice of the Grand Master from the British Taekwondo Foundation penetrates the Ladies' room. She hears him welcoming them, wishing them luck. Her fingers become clumsier.

Finally, the correct knot takes shape. Crumbs under bare feet, she stands in front of the mirror, pulls her hair into a neat ponytail and quickly reapplies lip gloss. *You got this, girl.*

Exiting the Ladies', she can feel the trailing crumbs. She steadies herself on the door handle, rubs one foot against her trousers, then the other. She opens the door.

The judges' table is set up right outside the changing room. She bows to the five judges, and to Master, who is too preoccupied to be fussed about her lateness. She slinks along the wall, then takes a seat on the floor with fellow students. There will be a few good minutes before she's called.

She straddles wide, stretches over each leg, rests her chest on the floor. She twists her torso in each direction, rotates her bad ankle clockwise, then counter. She picks a crumb from the tape on her foot, then cups her hands around shimmery blue toenails. She's glad that, unlike in competitions, she didn't need to remove her polish.

Minutes seem like hours as she sits, soles together, flapping her knees, twiddling the strap of her helmet. *Breathe.*

'Estelle,' Master finally calls.

After months of exam training (all those sacrificed weekends!), this is it.

Stella makes room for the fluttering as she takes her place, front and centre of the panel. The lower belts line up behind her, feet in position, hands clasped behind backs.

Poomsaes are first – patterns of movements against an invisible enemy.

It's just a performance, she recites silently, *you know what to do.* Poomsaes are choreographed, after all.

Master calls out *Si-jak,* and it's show time.

The first form is the gentlest, and it feels like sailing through a cool breeze. She picks up speed with the second, as does her heartbeat.

Then it happens.

When Stella gets into that zone, nothing else exists. Her punches sharp, kicks high, stances solid, she performs the remaining six patterns without missing a beat.

The others bow and sit down while she continues with the advanced forms required for Second Dan black belts.

There's no more sailing now.

The final form signifies a 'hardness', that which is too strong to be broken. That of a mighty warrior. This is what Stella needs to be now. She feels it in her muscle memory. She feels it in her bones.

Hot-faced and short-breathed, she sits down in disbelief. This is the first time she has executed her patterns with such precision. A fellow student pats her on the back. She sits, but not for long. No time to catch her breath, her butterflies. No time to check her ankle, her elbow.

Self-defence techniques are next. She's rehearsed these every day for months. She's even paired with her practice partner. It should all be predictable and smooth. Instead, it's fumbly and awkward. Her partner's wrists are sweaty and slip from her grip too easily.

She manages the takedowns in fluid, rapid succession. Until her ankle twitches. She stumbles, and the rotation of the throw nearly causes her to fall with her partner. She looks to Master, gives him a coy smile and shrugs. He nods, encourages her to carry on.

Yet uncertainty rushes back in, hijacking any lingering exhilaration.

She sits back down, a sinking feeling – no, a shrinking feeling – inside.

The exam goes on and on.

There are fitness challenges. Kicking drills up and down the gym, to the point of breathlessness.

More sitting.

There are power challenges. Board breaking with elbows, feet and fists to the point of pain.

More sitting.

Sparring is last. Her butterflies are in a frenzy now, even after nearly four hours. She tightens the Velcro of shin and arm guards, her uniform clinging to sweaty skin. She inserts her gum shield, swallowing the initial gag, and notices her hand is trembling.

Her ankle throbs, as does her face, when she stands to fasten her helmet. The pain shoots up her calf like a dart. The adrenaline helps her ignore all this.

How she wishes her husband would be home, to draw an ice-cold bath. To elevate her leg with cushions. To run the massage gun across achy shoulders. But she can't think about that, or the little moving plane over the Atlantic, or anything else right now, or she'll get kicked in the face.

Blood pulses in her ears as she takes her place on the blue square. She bows to her partner, the hotshot kid. Stella circles him, bouncing on her feet, anticipating, dodging. He's younger, but she's faster. She also has a few demons that require release.

She doesn't break eye contact. Not once.

She finally knows how to handle bullies.

I release myself from my past.

They taunt each other with a few fake-out kicks. She shifts back, dodges a side-kick. But the turning-kick that follows lands hard on her stomach, nearly winding her.

There's a feeling of surprise, even hurt at first. But this is a gift.

Her body turns hotter, and the butterflies morph into something wild, foreign yet familiar. It rises up fast in her, like a phoenix. It steadies her, propels her.

This urge, this instinct, is to charge him like an animal. To tackle him to the ground, pummel him relentlessly.

But she's worked too hard for this.

I release myself.

I am strong. I am present.

I am in control.

She collects herself – *breathe, Stella, breathe* – and resumes her bounce. Her face is on fire, her lips are tight, her eyes glassy. She shouts and goes in for a headshot, knocking his helmet askew with her instep.

A split-second freeze between them.

There's no releasing her lock on his eyes. She reads embarrassment, maybe intimidation, in them. Predator has become prey.

He retaliates with a back-kick. She anticipates this, side-shifts clear.

A few more close calls. No more points shots. The round goes fast.

They shake hands and return to the side-lines, breathing hard.

But something has yet to be satiated. Her eyes follow her panting quarry. She notices a slight limp in his gait.

A student releases him from his body armour. He sits with a thud.

Stella's descent to the floor is slow, controlled. There's power in it. She could go another round, play with him some more. She removes her helmet, hair sticking to her forehead. She removes her gum shield, a string of spit follows. Eyes on the hotshot, she wipes her mouth on her sleeve, then gulps from her water.

A student next to her is saying something, but she can't hear him.

Now new wings beat against her sore stomach. Her eyes search for reassurance, volleying from the judges to her Master stationed behind them.

Master finally looks over. With his nod, a cage door opens.

All butterflies are released.

///deny.rare.quarrel
by Billy Green

Now

'The problem is you don't want to work,' Eddie slurred, zipping up his flies. 'Here, here, here… I'll tell you what, I'll give you this dollar,' he unrolled one from a gold clip, 'if you can tell me why you don't have a job, eh?' He waved it back and forth slowly in front of the homeless man's eyes.

Eddie pulled up the collar on his Burberry cashmere car coat, a barrier against the harsh bite of the driving sleet. The man sat silently at his feet. He held a cardboard sign:

My name is Steve. I am a veteran. Please give as little as you can. Thank you and God Bless.

Eddie took a pull on a silver hip flask, newly engraved with *Salesman of the Year 1999*. He proffered it down to Steve.

'No? Trying to give up, eh?' Eddie said. 'Good man, good man.'

The Times Square clock flickered between *01:00* and *-12 Degrees*. A faint hint of fireworks hung in the air, a whiff of sulphur frozen in the mizzle. Ticker tape was stranded in gutters. The paper strips formed tentative bridges over the bars of the drains studding the centre of the alley off Broadway.

Steve's beard held tiny jewels of frost, gems adorning a face devoid of any wealth.

Then

Eddie didn't know Steve's pain, didn't know Steve had written in his diary only that morning, about January 1991, three months into a tour of Iraq during the first Gulf War. If Eddie cared he could have picked up the diary at Steve's side, read the pages laid open, his heart bare:

'We had gradually made our way North from Basra, Danny and I, travelling across 930 kilometres of battle-scarred sand. Across almost the whole length of Iraq, we had seen more action in those three months than the whole of our careers to date put together. We arrived just after each advance, our Land Rover and trailer accompanied by an escort of either the US Airborne Division or the Royal Marines of 3 Commando Brigade.

On arrival, we would set up the communications so the officers could receive orders from HQ. The communications were also used for calling wives and/or girlfriends, so we became very popular very quickly, often given extra rations in exchange for airtime. But it wasn't the smell of sausage and beans or creamy beef stew that lingered, it was the rank odour of decay from the bodies, the sun accelerating the journey from the corpses to our noses and mouths, death hanging onto the clothes and webbing belts even once the bodies had gone.

And the heat was intense, dry and energy-sapping for fourteen hours of each day before the freezing cold of the night, never resting at a comfortable temperature. We couldn't sleep so we welcomed the distraction of having to clean the sand that crept into the tiniest of gaps, weapons needing dry cleaning each evening, equipment blown through each morning before use with a portable vacuum cleaner. We were busy every second of every day, and after three months the fatigue was hitting us all, judgements becoming more snapped and less considered.

As well as the heat, the atmosphere hung tight with tension. From morning to night we were coiled taut. You could see it in the way our colleagues walked across the camp, shoulders tensed, heads jerking at the slightest noise – a breeze rattling a can along the dust path, a fallen twig snapping underfoot. The towns we slept in and the seemingly endless roads that led us to them were boobytrapped by the fleeing locals, unwilling to leave anything to the invaders. And like the glass of water that is carried for ten minutes, one hour, two hours and eventually becomes more than just a simple vial of liquid, we became heavy with the stress. We were as nomadic as the expelled natives, homeless and holding tight to our meagre possessions, boots and cots becoming high-value currency, held as close to us as our weapons.

That week in Mosul was the toughest of the tour. We were told that the very specific, apparently high-profile targets were holed up in a safe house that had been identified by an Iraqi informant. The task of capture was given to 101st Airborne Division. The history books tell the story better than I can. The task was successful, depending on your definition of success.

As the action died down, Danny and I set up a satellite link from the house, so the team leader could report back in situ that the area had been cleared, made safe. While Major Tom Lightman – the tall, rangy officer in command – called in his report, Danny and I looked around the house and garden. As we stepped through the fallen wreckage of the balcony that had circumnavigated the interior courtyard, Danny saw something glinting in the sand, the sun directly overhead and coincidental to our passing.

We knelt and brushed away the earth from around the object and found it to be a tiny gold statue, a god on a chariot, no bigger than three inches tall and five inches wide. It was chipped and tarnished with age, but I guess that was why we knew it might be worth something. I looked at Danny and Danny looked at me, holding each other's gaze for a second or so, Danny eventually nodding slightly as I gently shook my head. Danny removed his glove from his right hand and picked up the treasure in his dirt ingrained thumb and forefinger, turned it over and held it in his palm, mesmerised.

Suddenly, the remainder of an arched wooden door tipped from its ruined hinges. An Iraqi man, clad in a thawb and shmakh, stood looking at the idol in Danny's hand, a frown crossing his brow and his mouth opening to shout.

'Contact!' Danny screamed on impulse, panicking, alerting the sentry outside. We didn't see the hair-trigger of the M4 Carbine pulled, but we heard the shot and saw the Iraqi fall through the doorway. Danny didn't look at me, he pocketed the statue and walked silently back into the house. And as usual I followed him.

A year later, back in the UK, we met in London. The sky had darkened to a slate grey, rain was threatening to fall and the wind gusting down Edgeware Road portended a storm ahead. Huddled together in a studded leather booth at the Green Man in Paddington, Danny handed me an envelope. I opened it and counted out one thousand five hundred pounds. Danny had sold the treasure at Northgate Road Antiques Market in Battersea that afternoon. He explained that after some casual questioning about the source of the idol, the owner had led Danny through to a back room and counted out the money in fifty-pound notes. Danny coloured in the story with detail that made it sound even more implausible than the amount of cash offered. Three thousand pounds, the man's life had been worth three thousand pounds. And as we shared everything during that tour, I took the money.

I still haven't spent it. It might even still sit in a desk in the spare room; I only took it to share Danny's pain. Danny couldn't handle the pain. He fell in front of a train three months later. A week after that I moved to New York and left the money in the house for the landlord to find, a payment to ease my guilt. But the guilt never goes.

Now

'Yes, the war was horrible. Well, *boo hoo*,' Eddie said. 'I was away two weeks out of every four this year, flying across twenty states. Sometimes the room wasn't cleaned for days, the same filthy sheets night after night. And I had to share them some nights, know what I mean, eh, eh?' Eddie nudged an elbow in the air, laughing at the memory of drunken fumbles under motel duvets, sometimes free, sometimes on expenses.

The salesman pulled a battered pack of Marlboro Lights from his fur-lined pocket, tapped one into the crook between his finger and thumb, then pushed it clumsily into his mouth.

'You want one? No, giving up, eh? Good man, good man,' Eddie said, impressed with Steve's stoicism. 'No, no, no . . . wait, let me finish. I know it's hard.' He bent over at the waist now, speaking more softly. 'I know it's hard, but you should get out there, put yourself about, you know? Be useful.'

Eddie moved his hand to pat Steve's shoulder but missed and stumbled, twisting to one side, left shoulder coming over the top of his right. He caught himself at the last moment, missed Steve, and pulled himself upright.

The snow fell harder, drifting on the lids of bins against brick walls, like sea foam from a warmer place. Discarded flyers eddied along the corridor, sweeping in circles along its length before becoming trapped, flat out against the mesh of the wire fence blocking the far end. Voices swirled, high-pitched screams against the wind, directions shouted for the next bar. The blast of air would be felt from the vents above the doors, pins and needles emerging with the change in temperature. But the breeze persisted in the alley, and Eddie persevered with Steve.

'Nothing to say, eh? Cat got your tongue?' Eddie put the dollar back in his pocket. 'Well, you're not getting this then.' He spat, straightened, and meandered away, haloed by the lights of Broadway.

The veteran's eyes remained frozen open. His hand remained outstretched. He'd been like that for an hour now. Since his heart slowed. Slowed, slowed. Stuttered and stopped.

///cure.brings.tribe
by Catherine Johnstone

I didn't live with my girlfriend, Max. Our relationship was a murky combination of independence and commitment. At her place that night, she made a slab of toffee for the crème brûlée. It was burnt but she served it up anyway. I was going to a Queer Masked Ball later, but Max didn't want to come. While I got dressed at her place, the burnt taste lingered in my mouth. I thought she wanted to break up with me, but whenever I asked her what was going on, she said, 'Nothing.'

That night I stayed in my friend Ash's spare room because it was walking distance from the ball. As Ash and I strolled over there, it felt strange to be out without Max. My chest hurt as though I was wearing a chest-binder. I looked down at my second-hand black pants, white shirt and black waistcoat. I straightened my bowtie. I wasn't in the mood to inhabit these clothes as if I was someone else, pretending to be a tough butch. Ash skittered beside me; her baby-dyke face the same as it was at uni all those years ago. I dangled a spangly $2 mask in my hand.

The sign 'Queerlesque Masquerade Ball' was decorated with painted masks and hung above the Collingwood Town Hall's front door. I recognised a voice in the entrance queue. It was Jac.

I'd met them at the gender workshop but didn't know if they would remember me. I reminded myself to use 'they' and 'them' instead of 'she'. I straightened my shoulders. It was the first time I'd been to a major queer event. I can do this, I thought. I bit a flake of skin on my bottom lip.

'Hey, Jac,' I said.

They spun around. The yellow and purple mask flipped upwards obscuring her, I mean, their, eyes. They lowered the mask and peered through the eyeholes.

'Hey,' Jac said. 'I remember. We met at the workshop.' They indicated the person lolling beside them. 'This is my friend Shell. Shell, this is Tee.'

Shell flashed a smile showing silver mesh on her teeth.

I introduced Ash. Jac shook her hand, the arrow tattoo on their upper arm moving as the muscles flexed.

'C'mon, Jac. Let's go.' Shell grabbed Jac's arm and pulled them forwards in the queue.

I put my mask on as I stepped inside the hall. A net filled with blinking lights was suspended from one end of the upper balcony to the other. A catwalk extended into the hall from the stage at the far end. Music blared. Lights flickered on a sea of gyrating arms, legs and masked faces. People of all genders wore formal wear, sequins, casual gear, glittering outfits, shorts; everything was possible. It didn't matter if you were omnigender, genderqueer, a yet-to-be-discovered-letter-in-the-acronym, male or female. I loved the mix of people. The room had an edgy vibe, tinged with a metallic smell. I wanted to leap into the freedom of this unknown.

Ash darted off to say hello to a friend waving her arms in the air. I threaded my way towards the drinks queue. Jac stood nearby, shoulders jerking to the music in a T-shirt with torn-off sleeves.

I straightened my back, trying to appear confident. 'Wanna dance?'

Through the mask, they held my eyes, inviting me in. 'Later. Shell's getting beers.' Their eyes travelled down my body. 'Love the outfit.'

I hadn't felt attracted to anyone since I met Max. Don't go there, I thought.

The music quietened. A drag queen MC paraded onto the stage in purple shoes. She had beehive hair, and her low-cut dress was ruched above her knees in front and down to her heels at the back.

'Welcome, guys, gals and non-binary pals!' she shouted. 'This is our fabulous Queerlesque show! Are we all having a good time?' She thrust out her arms to the audience and cupped an ear for a response.

Half-hearted *yeahs* sounded throughout the hall.

'I didn't hear that,' she yelled into her mic.

Loud yells of 'Yes!' and 'Yeah!' reverberated.

'What are we?' she asked.

Everyone looked confused and one screamed, 'Trans!'

Some people smiled.

'Queer by birth, fabulous by choice.' The MC pounded out the slogan.

'What are we?' she yelled again.

'Queer by birth, fabulous by choice.' The chorus reverberated around the hall and sent shivers up and down my arms. I felt connected to the freedom of these people, the openness to being themselves.

'Welcome to our first performer,' the MC said. 'The majestic Matto Mojo de Morny. Backing music by Momo.'

Applause erupted as classical music mixed with electric guitar and drums blasted into the hall. Matto Mojo strutted along the stage and onto the catwalk, sliding sultry looks in all directions. Her blue trench coat reached to her calves and was printed with pink mouths, each with a beckoning tongue. With each flouncing step, Matto pulled the coat zip downwards with a provocative look. Each time the zip was pulled down, the A string of a cello shrilled out a note. The crowd catcalled and hooted. The hall smelt of sweat and excitement.

Someone touched my arm. It was Jac. Their fist nudged around my stomach and stopped in front of my navel. They uncurled their fingers while I watched, hypnotised. People clapped and yelled around us. In the middle of Jac's palm was a pink pill with a raised star.

'What is it?' I asked.

'E,' Jac said. Through one of the eyeholes, I made out a wink.

I sneaked a look around. No-one was watching. Not that it mattered. Half the crowd was probably on E too. I nodded, swallowed the pill with a gulp of red, and Jac disappeared through the crowd.

Ash pushed towards me and handed me another red wine. I didn't know if I should drink more wine after an E but I accepted it anyway.

After Matto's performance, the DJ took over, playing a bracket of women's songs. I found Ash to tell her I'd decided to go home early. My hand shook and wine slopped over the side of my glass. I'll rest first, I thought. I wandered over to a staircase at the end of the room and climbed up. At the top was a hallway with ornate cornices and arched windows. I sank to the carpet behind a pillar and sipped my wine, mask dangling off one ear.

My mind jingled. My pelvis hummed. The wine tasted like blackberries and plums and dark chocolate. The music pounded. Aretha demanded respect, Petula suggested going downtown and Madonna told me to stand alone, and she'll take me there. Like Gloria, I was afraid, no, I was petrified but Reddy roared I was invincible.

Someone strode up the stairs. Madonna's power in the midnight hour. Jac smoothed their palm across mine, my other hand still holding the wine. My stomach somersaulted. They placed my glass on the uneven carpet. It wobbled and tipped over, leaving a stain that might become permanent.

I sat beside Jac in the taxi's back seat. It was 4am. Our thighs jostled as we turned corners. I leaned my head against the glass, pretending a leg wasn't touching mine. A light blinked on a verandah, an electric scooter whizzed by with an UberEats bag bouncing on the back. Jac's thigh was warm. Lights pulsed. Hardware store window, McDonald's window, Repair Shop window. Fences and houses blurred. People inside were making love, dreaming of making love. Someone ate an early morning snack before work. I wanted an early morning snack. A warm body Jac snack. A creamy porridge with ripe red strawberries Jac snack. A poached-eggs-gleaming, yolk-spilling, hollandaise-dribbling Jac snack.

It was all very well to dream, but this was what happened. When we arrived, Jac guided me into their apartment. It was dark. I tripped over boots in the hallway. They turned on the light and led me into the kitchen.

'Want a drink?'

'Water, thanks.'

Jac handed me a glass and I sipped while they watched me. They grabbed my hand and led me into their bedroom. My pelvis pulsed and I wanted to say yes, *yes, yes.*

We sat on the bed, and someone spun in the air between us. Max blurred before my E-shining eyes and I said, 'I can't. Can I sleep on the couch?'

'Sure.' Jac brought me a doona decorated with fairies.

I was awake for hours, every cell longing to dart into the bedroom. My mind and body wrestled. I told myself; I have a partner. We agreed to be monogamous. Things weren't perfect, but I resolved to find out what was going on with her tomorrow. I thought, no, no, no.

When I was back at the flat, Max sent me a brief text. *Things aren't working out. I don't think we should see each other anymore.* And just like that it was over.

I felt disconnected from my body. A few glasses of gin and tonic might help, I thought, so I downed three. When I picked up the third drink, it slipped from my hand and crashed on the floor. As I cleaned it up, a sliver of glass gashed my palm.

I rang Jac but there was no answer.

I concentrated on my cut hand, trying to feel the pain, to get back to my body.

When I tried Jac again, they answered the phone straight away.

I mumbled, 'Can I see you?'

'Pardon?'

I repeated myself.

'Now?'

'Yep.'

'Where are you?' Jac asked.

'Home in Preston.'

'Can you get to the Cornwall in Brunswick?'

'Yep,' I mumbled. 'I'll get an Uber.'

'See you there in half an hour.'

I gulped two glasses of water, rang an Uber and lurched out the door. My mind was loud, my edges frayed.

At the doorway of the Cornwall bar, I felt disoriented. I peeked inside. It was dim with velvety curtains around the walls and smelt of spilt beer and musty fabric. Groups of people were clustered around high tables, each illuminated by the glow from an old-fashioned lampshade. Everyone focussed on a man out the front reading a question. When he finished, voices broke out around the room.

Jac glanced at the cut on my hand. 'You okay?'

I shrugged. Jac led me to a dark corner at the back.

'Want a drink?'

'Gin and tonic. Thanks.'

Jac returned, two drinks held with slender fingers that tapered towards bitten off fingernails. If they touched my hand, would it bring me back to my body, my bones, my skin?

I rested one forearm on the high table. Then I placed it in my lap. Jac's spiky green hair shone even in the dim light at the back of the room. Jac green hair, Jac gleaming eyes, Jac fingers. I put my forearm back on the table. I couldn't believe we were here. I rested my arm back in my lap. My face felt flushed. The MC called out a question and people around each table bent in to chat.

Jac's eyes gleamed as they gazed towards the MC up the front. 'Stonewall.'

'What?'

'The answer.' Jac flashed a cheeky grin.

I studied the people and realised it was a queer crowd. 'Is this a queer trivia night?'

'Yeah. Thursday night is queer night. It's not always Trivia though.'

A person yelled out 'Nevo Zisin' and someone said, 'Don't tell the whole room.'

The MC asked another, but I concentrated on my breath, alert to this spark with Jac.

'Queer as folk,' Jac whispered, flicking fingers through their hair. As their hand flew in slow motion back to their beer, I wished it would alight on my upturned palm like a honeyeater.

The atmosphere buzzed. 'I've never been here before,' I said.

'You don't get out much, I guess.' Jac nudged my shoulder.

Jac rearranged their face into a 'time for a serious subject' look. 'How's it going with your partner?'

'Not good.'

We were silent for a few minutes.

A bubble of froth glistened in the corner of their lips, and they licked it off. '2017.'

'What was the question?' I asked.

'The year same-sex marriage was legalised in Australia.'

I surprised myself with a jokey tone. 'Fount of all knowledge you are.' I grinned and flicked their shoulder. 'Want another beer?'

Jac grabbed hold of my hand and squeezed it. My blood hummed.

'Cocktail, thanks,' Jac said.

I grabbed my wallet and heaved myself up. Jac whispered in my ear as if it was an endearment. 'Courtney.'

Did Jac get my name wrong? 'Is that a cocktail?'

'No, silly, a celebrity whose last name is Act.'

My face flamed.

'Manhattan.' Jac grinned.

I smiled back. 'You're a tease. I know that's a cocktail.'

I walked to the bar, limbs loosened by the gin and the atmosphere. This floatiness was tilting me towards euphoria.

I handed Jac their honey-coloured cocktail glittering with ice. They put the glass on the table and touched my palm. My hand was damp from condensation and theirs was warm. The ice cubes crackled in the glass and my skin burned.

'Thanks, hon,' they said.

Hon? I sat down, grasping my gin and tonic.

Jac set the Manhattan on the table, reached for my hand and turned it over. They ran their finger across the skin from thumb to forefinger. My body tingled as if my veins were having an effervescent party. I was here. My body was here.

I looked up at the MC, unsure whether to take my hand away or not. I picked up my drink with the other. 'I know this one.'

'What?'

'Leslie Feinberg.'

They grinned. 'You stone butch you. Come here.'

I sipped my drink and edged closer to Jac. Through my shirt, they traced the shape of my spine. Skin, bumps of vertebrae and ropes of muscle vibrated at their touch. I plonked my glass on the table with a bang.

I fizzed with heat, haze, gin. Max's face swam away from me. I floated in a new sea. My hand searched for skin beneath Jac's flannelette shirt.

They pulled away and yelled, 'Pink, white and blue.'

A deep voice yelled, 'Thanks.'

'I know. Trans flag,' I said.

'Good one.'

I glowed at the praise. At least I got one right.

'I don't even know what work you do,' I said.

'It's boring. I work in a call centre. All about your gas bill.'

'Gas?'

'Yeah, it's like this.' Jac adopted a formal tone as they met my eyes. 'What is your full name, please?'

I hesitated.

'Go on, answer,' Jac said in a mock-bossy voice.

'Teresa Bernadette Ryan.'

I'm such an obedient name-answerer, like a twelve-year-old who thinks she'll go to hell if she doesn't tell the truth, the whole truth and nothing but.

Jac pursed her lips as if to hide a smile. 'Date of birth?' Beneath the table, their hand flicked around the top of my thighs. Oh my God, what was going on? Could I resist this?

'24th September 1979.' I sipped my drink. Drops dribbled down my chin.

'Did you listen to the privacy statement?' They held my gaze while their hand found its way inside the waistband of my jeans and crept downwards.

'Yes, no, yes, not here.' My inhalation was audible.

'Sure?'

'No, not sure. Here, here.'

'Hear, hear.'

I sizzled.

'Do you have a gas stove or a gas heater?'

'Heater,' I gasped.

'Do you like the temperature turned up high?'

'Yeah,' I panted.

We burst into a fit of giggling. I'd almost forgotten the freedom of laughter. Their hand slipped away, but my body simmered like sugar melting on the stovetop, caramelised and unburnt.

///footsteps.scowls.embers
by Nina Smith

Hannah always ran like she was being chased. She would pick a landmark – a tree, a woman pushing a stroller – about two hundred yards ahead on the cobbled footpath that serpentined its way around Tirana's main lake, and sprint as though outrunning a predator. She'd seek him out in crowds but felt his presence more when she was alone. She constantly looked over her shoulder for him, but never saw his face. Still, she knew the shape of him. A hulking figure. Dark clothes. A hungry, menacing smile. He was a figment of her imagination, born from years of confronting news headlines and weathered warnings, exacerbated by her own nightmares. He was no-one yet could be anyone.

Each time she reached her target, Hannah pushed herself to sprint for a few more seconds and then slowed to a jog, allowing herself to catch her breath. She then set off again. Same routine, different landmark. An old man, dressed in a dusty tweed suit despite the scorching summer heat, sitting on an upturned crate and nursing a bottle of homemade raki. A stray dog basking in the dappled sunlight beneath an oak tree. Every turn around the irregular contours of the lake felt like she was uncovering a new fresco, each more colourful and chaotic than the last.

The lake spread out through the centre of Tirana's main park. Reflected on the water's glistening surface was a densely packed formation of Balkan trees and botanicals, interrupted with the occasional slice of new construction, mostly hotels and apartments to accommodate the country's burgeoning tourism industry. They called the lake the 'lungs of the city.' And that's what it felt like to Hannah, like each stride oxygenated the tension in her veins, dispelling it with endorphin-fuelled relief. The bustling presence of locals going about their business, walking in all directions, often directly in her path, filled Hannah with a sense of calm. Maybe it was that she could get lost within the crowds. Maybe it was that she felt safer surrounded by witnesses.

She revelled in the temporary break that running afforded her. That's why she did it. It softened the effects of the fears and anxieties that had seeped through her spinal cord and implanted themselves into other parts of her body, the intrusive thoughts like tiny parasites. Her chest felt tight, her shoulders were always tense and, when she ran, she realised she'd been breathing without really *breathing*. If she went more than a few days without running, she'd bite her fingernails down to their nubs before realising she was doing it. This all eased when she ran, particularly now she was on the other side of Europe. She'd heard of people letting go of their senses when on holiday somewhere foreign, emboldened with a false sense of security. When she jogged around the lake, she could understand why. Sometimes she'd go two, three minutes without looking behind her. Progress.

Hannah had arrived in Albania two months earlier. Two weeks extended into four weeks extended into an indefinite stay. Outwardly, she was a digital nomad who'd uprooted herself from the pallor of corporate London life to work as a freelancer

whilst exploring the last remaining Balkan jewel. It sounded
carefree and hedonistic, the actions of someone with an
insatiable thirst for exploration and adventure. Inwardly, she
was running. From bad habits, poor choices, and a self-
destructive appetite for ascending the corporate ladder at the
expense of everything that stood not just in her path, but slightly
to the side of it, too. Relationships would incend and fizzle out.
Enduring friendships became pockmarked by distance. Even her
family had stopped inviting her to gatherings, knowing she was
unlikely to turn up. She used to wear her burnout like a badge
of honour. Smashing targets and being given promotions fuelled
her. Until it didn't.

She was checking her messages as she walked towards the
train station late one evening, a route so familiar it was
practically etched into the fibres of her leg muscles. At precisely
the same moment that she closed an email from her well-
meaning sister (*You can't go on like this, Han. Something's gotta
give.*), she'd walked into oncoming traffic. Luckily, the traffic
was just a car with a prudent driver slowly pulling out of his
spot, so her injuries were minor. The bonnet had barely kissed
her kneecaps, but the fright had caused her to tumble
backwards, warranting a visit to the Emergency Department
and an accompanying lecture from the nurse taking her blood
pressure (elevated, of course) about being present and in the
moment. The incident looked worse than it was. It was nothing
really. But as she signed out of the hospital reception, uttering
more promises about work-life balance that would inevitably be
broken, she felt the gaze of another eye on her. It was umpteen
shades of a deep and captivating blue. Too bright to be human,
it summoned her to bathe in its azure waters.

The piercing depths of the eye drowned out the nurse's
sermon on *slowing down*.

'Where's that?' Hannah asked, pointing over the receptionist's shoulder mid-sentence.

'That? That's *Syri i Kaltër*. The Blue Eye. It's in Albania,' the nurse said, clearly rattled that Hannah wasn't even pretending to drink in her sage lecture. 'You should go. It might do you some good.'

Hannah had never been impulsive, so perhaps it was the shock of the crash-that-wasn't-a-crash, but that night she looked up Albania and by the time she'd finished the fifth clickbait-headlined article about the country (*Seven reasons a trip to Albania will change your life forever!*), her flight was booked.

Now, she found herself in a beautiful Balkan purgatory. She hadn't realised at the time, but embarking that plane marked the end of one chapter and the start of the next. Two weeks had evolved into something more enduring.

A cloud of cicadas chirruped somewhere over her head in a loud percussive thrum, and she looked over her shoulder again.

Day in, day out, she jogged at least one lap of the lake, sometimes three or four. It's not like she had anything better to do. No client briefings, no internal meetings. No working lunches, industry shindigs, drinks with clients. Now, a working day was comprised of the occasional Zoom call to discuss the creative requirements of whichever client was paying her that day followed by a few hours hunched over her laptop. That was enough to keep her living comfortably here (one of the headlines she'd read on the night she booked her flights was '*Live like a king on the budget of a pauper!*'). She was far removed from her previous life and all its banal comforts and predictabilities and disappointments. Her uniform of heels and suits had been replaced with jeans and sneakers, her sleek blow-dried bob with tendrils plastered across her forehead by sweat. It was a complete change of scene, and she still didn't know how she felt about it. Still staggered by her own impulsiveness, mostly, but there was also something else. Amidst the transient sense of unease (did she ever not feel this, she wondered), it felt like a weight had lifted, just slightly. It felt as though the distance from her old life had stripped it of some of its meaning. The shimmer had faded from her soaring career trajectory. Her goals had lost their potency. She didn't know where this chapter would lead, but she knew with startling clarity she couldn't go back. So, onwards she ran.

Hannah had almost completed her first lap around the lake and passed a small grove of ancient olive trees, their mottled roots so intertwined it would be impossible for even the trees themselves to decipher which branch belonged where. This was a quieter part of the course, the hubbub of people sticking to the part more heavily lined with cafés and the promise of sustenance.

She'd stop when she reached the next row of cafés, she decided. Water first, then coffee. Just another quarter lap. You never had to walk far for a brew in Albania, the consumption of coffee so ingrained in the culture, it bore more reverence than any religion. No transaction or interaction, no matter how menial, was undertaken without a shot of fine, Italian espresso. She'd really taken to this custom and now punctuated her days with a multitude of coffee breaks.

She pushed herself to keep her pace, could feel her heartbeat rising but knew it would do her good. She was wiping sweat away from her sodden hairline when she caught a movement behind her. There was a certainty in the movement, a purpose that made it feel as though someone had blown cold air onto the sweat pooling at the base of her neck. She kept running but looked back again. A man, not fifty yards away, was running towards her. Tall, broad shoulders swathed in dark clothes. She was hyper aware that nobody else was around, not behind him nor in front of her.

Hannah pressed her elbows to her sides. She quickened her pace. Just a few hundred yards and round the bend, and she'd be back in the safety net of a crowd. *Keep running.* When she looked back again, he was sprinting, and though she couldn't see clearly, she felt his eyes burning a target onto her body. There was a frightening intent in his stride. She picked up her pace, gaining momentum with each step. Her breathing intensified.

She felt like a doe with the laser sight of a hunting rifle searing into her back.

Breathe, she told herself. *Just keep running.*

She was sprinting now. She didn't dare look back again for fear of losing milliseconds that could save her life, but she could sense him gaining on her with each step.

Each time she upped her speed, she heard his cadence increase too. She felt him close the gap with each strike of his feet on the cobblestones below.

She cast about for places she could escape, but it was a 300-yard stretch of bush-lined path in front of her, and not another person in sight. If she veered off into the shrub, she'd be trapped. She heard his pounding footsteps come closer still.

She knew she couldn't outrun him now, yet she persisted, propelling herself forward, determined to get away from this man, this manifestation of a stranger that had haunted her fears for a decade. Some version of him had been coming for her since breasts had sprouted from the flat planes of her chest. She'd hit puberty young, and her sense of awkwardness came not from her shifting silhouette but from the perceptible alteration in the way people, mostly men, observed her and the new, uncomfortable undercurrent to these interactions that she wouldn't understand until years later. Yes, she'd always known this day would come. It had been as inevitable as her first menstrual cycle.

She'd be among the crowds again in moments. She just needed to reach the next corner. She could see the sun reflecting off the smooth cobblestones ahead, the warmth of the light summoning her to safety.

Just a hundred more yards. Hannah looked back again, and he was just steps away now. She could hear his breath, certain and rhythmic. She found herself start to slow, unable to keep the momentum.

She could practically feel his breath on her neck.

She then heard his voice, closer still, threatening and deep, as he shouted something from behind her.

Hannah screamed, a reflexive, guttural cry. Rather than her life flashing before her eyes, a plethora of grotesque events played out in her mind as he closed the gap and she braced for impact. She saw herself being pushed to the ground. A hand covering her mouth before another scream could leave her lips. A thigh pressing into her groin. Her arms held down until the fight was extinguished out of her.

But none of these grisly scenarios would transpire.

He sprinted past her, and not looking back, shouted again, something in Albanian. Then he laughed. There was a mocking tone in his timbre.

She scowled as she keeled over and gasped for air, her face reddening. She could feel her heartbeat thrumming in her neck, quick and mad. She caught her breath as he put more distance between them. She looked up and noticed he'd slowed his pace, having proved his physical superiority. He joined a group of young men, wearing the same dark sweater, a uniform of some sort. She hadn't noticed them before but they now stood like a mirage beaming up from a spread of wet cobblestones just yards ahead. They high-fived their team member as he joined their swarm, and then ran around the next bend and out of sight.

Once Hannah could breathe properly again, she continued jogging. She stopped when she reached the café that in just a short time had ensconced itself as her favourite, and ordered the bottle of water she needed and the shot of espresso she craved. She sat at what had become her usual table and drank in the sights in front of her, of locals going about their day. Her heart rate returned to normal, imbuing her with a wash of relief.

As she finished her drinks and headed off for one last lap of the lake, Hannah reflected on the words the man had shouted after he passed her. His laughter was still ringing in her ears. She didn't yet have a strong hold of the Albanian language, so could only guess what he'd said. *Crazy woman*, he'd implied. Crazy for being so afraid. Perhaps he was right. Perhaps she had overreacted. But perhaps he told his girlfriend not to run alone after five p.m. Perhaps he asked his sister to text him once she got to her friend's house. And perhaps he chaperoned his mother on her walk home whenever she came to his place for dinner.

Yes, she was crazy alright. Crazy for thinking she could leave *everything* behind in London. Just like the anxieties from which this unknown yet familiar predator was born, the fear of him would always be there, lurking in the shadowy depths of her imagination. But, if she was lucky, he'd never move beyond that.

///relay.final.voices
by Emile Cassen

Sophie arrives early for her first visit. She steps out of the chaos of Fulham Palace Road – the crowds, diesel fumes, cyclists and joggers – into the relative serenity of the hospital foyer. A man sits at a piano with a brightly painted 'Play me' sign. Next to him, a woman holding a drip stand sings '. . . in the stillness of remembering what you had . . . and what you lost,' her fragile breathy voice adding a haunting quality to their performance.

Sophie's mind has been on hold, actively pushing out all thought, but the music allows in an unexpected rush of enthusiasm.

A small crowd has formed by the time a friendly face approaches and resolves itself into familiar features: blond hair, slightly chipped tooth, wearing grey as always. Elly. They embrace.

'Sorry I'm late,' then an outpouring of reasons Sophie doesn't hear, or hears but doesn't absorb. 'D'you know where we're going?'

She likes the 'we', as though they're on a social to a cinema, concert or bar. She pulls out the appointment letter again as they walk towards the floorplan. Fifteen cross-shaped floors, like a church. North Wing, South Wing, East Wing . . .

Elly frowns over her reading glasses, 'It isn't clear, is it? D'you think we're outpatients?

'Maybe. That would be Clinic Block. Here. First floor.'

A touch screen at the top of the escalator confirms their choice and directs them to waiting area D, a diffuse collection of chairs that seem to merge unnervingly with areas A to C.

'Let's sit here,' Elly says, pointing at two vacant seats.

Lab-coated figures bearing clipboards emerge sporadically from doors along the narrow corridors. They release patients, call out new names, help with wheelchairs, and arrange further appointments in the reception area. Finally, it's their turn and they're ushered into a small office. Sophie probes the consultant's face for distinguishing features for future reference; clean-shaven, young (maybe forties?), earnest grey eyes, but she knows this kind of cataloguing is proving increasingly unreliable. You can never quite capture the essence of a person.

The conversation is about Sophie.

'Me, my memory and . . . my . . . general disorientation,' she stammers, when he asks her if she knows what they're there to discuss.

The neurologist speaks to Sophie first, then to Elly.

'She does forget things sometimes, but really no more than I do,' Elly says.

Sophie is in danger of giggling; this all feels so farcical – they're talking about her in front of her – but the instructions were emphatic: 'You will need to bring a relative or friend who knows you well . . .' and no one knows her better. They've been friends since university, in and out of each other's homes throughout the years of child-rearing, propping each other up through betrayals, divorces, evictions and redundancies. They speak every day and tell each other everything.

The consultant is reassuring.

'It isn't uncommon to worry about dementia, especially if someone close to you is affected by it.'

In her case, it's her mother, and Sophie has just turned fifty, which is about the age that they noticed her mother's character started to change.

'From what you've told me – and from what I've seen of you today – I'd say you're just suffering from stress,' he says. 'We'll run some tests.'

The memory tests confirm her ropey recall, the psychological tests that she's anxious, and the MRI that her brain looks normal. It's all still pointing towards the long-term effects of stress, and Sophie is losing interest in this hospital, this doctor, and a diagnosis. She forgets why she came and what she was hoping to achieve, and there's always something better to do than hack across London to spend the best part of a day waiting here. But the consultant has one more test up his sleeve.

Sophie cancels it a few times for spurious reasons, then her father dies, and she has real cause to delay. More of her limited attention goes on what Alzheimer's has left of her mother, and it's the best part of two years later by the time she goes back to the hospital and allows the radioactive substance to course through her veins. Now she has a full-on job and it isn't easy to find time to get the results. She isn't the only one cancelling. The overstretched hospital cancels a few appointments too. Another year goes by before she returns for the result. Another two-hour wait, but at least this will be the last time. *I'm out of here*, she thinks.

Today, almost exactly three years since her first visit with Elly, she's sitting across the table from the same neurologist. He looks older, more rugged, and a little weary.

'So . . .' he says, his tone friendly, 'it's been quite a while. How have you been?' Something elusive overshadows his face. Is it concern? Incredulity? Has she forgotten some essential item of clothing? She scans downwards to check – all good – then clings to a conventional answer.

'Fine. Busy.'

'Symptoms?'

'The same really. I still don't feel right.'

'In what way?'

She reaches for a thought but finds only an increasingly familiar blankness. This will become panic if she doesn't think of something soon. Come up with an example. Quick. It doesn't have to be the best answer. Anything.

'It's little things. It isn't so much memory. It's more around people. I find social interactions overwhelming . . . and I struggle to recognise faces. A different expression looks like a different person to me.' She starts to relax a little. 'Even you just now. You passed me once in the corridor looking harassed. The next time you made eye contact and talked to me. To me that was two different people. Only your nametag gave you away. I've had whole conversations with people and not recognised them the next day...' Now she's rambling to cover up her embarrassment. This suddenly feels like a very a trivial reason to be taking up this specialist's precious time, but she can't put her finger on any other symptoms. Or maybe there are too many to choose from. Plenty of incidents have piled up, but she isn't inclined to direct her focus towards them.

'I really just came for the result of that scan.'

'No friend with you this time?'

'No, the letter didn't say...' But the real reason is that Elly's presence would have drained her. Not Elly specifically, but anyone. Thinking about what to say, worrying about what she was thinking, interpreting gestures.

She had felt a gaping absence in the foyer though, where they'd met on that first visit. She'd had a vague recollection that something had lifted her spirits there once, and she'd felt a little bereft that it was no longer there, whatever it was.

'Well...the scan's quite a cause for concern. Your brain has areas around here,' he demonstrates on his own head, 'where there's little or no metabolism. Look. This is a healthy brain'. He turns his computer screen slightly so that they can both see it. 'And this is your brain.'

'Wow! They're quite different. What does that bit of the brain do?'

'They're the parietal lobes. They process sensory information. It's an area where we often find metabolic impairments in early Alzheimer's, and atrophy here is one of the best early markers for the disease.' He clicks on another image. 'This is the brain of someone with Alzheimer's.' It is too similar to Sophie's.

Here's the thing. She can remember all these words. Parietal. Atrophy. Impairment. She knows what they've injected – [^{18}F] Fludeoxyglucose – she can draw its structure without thinking; a hexagonal glucose with the radioactive fluorine at C2 replacing the hydroxyl group. Homing in further, she knows more about these atoms – carbon, hydrogen, oxygen and fluorine – their properties, prevalence, even the latest theories about their subatomic makeup, than this doctor probably does. And it's almost self-explanatory to her how the PET scan works, how the distribution of [^{18}F] FDG shows where metabolism is taking place, and crucially, where it isn't.

All of this is no comfort to her. Her mother was trying to answer the phone by picking up a butter dish when she was still publishing papers on mathematical approaches to interfacial thermodynamics, so in this one area she was presumably still functioning effectively when everything else had fallen apart. Only later had Sophie found out how much effort it had cost her to hide the extent of her decline. On clearing the parental home, she'd found the stacks of notebooks her mother had kept, taking down the exact time and content of phone conversations, making copies of any letters and cards sent, and towards the end, writing her thoughts and feelings too, although sadly too few of these. By then the writing was wobbly and in places disjointed, but still recognisably her mother's.

Somewhat sombre. I can't play the piano anymore, or read books, or do physics. In short, there's hardly anything I can do, and I don't know what I can do about it.

It broke Sophie's heart to read, because it was her last coherent entry. After this, there was a page where she tried many times to write her own name, but each time she got stuck before the task was complete. Sophie could feel her fear and frustration.

Enid Davidso

Enid Da

Endi d

In a family where validity was found almost exclusively in the written word, it was especially poignant. It was official. Enid Davidson was no more.

What a sadistic disease this is, that slowly unravels a person's mind while they still have the capacity to watch it happen. No. It's worse than that, because before this intellectual decay, it chews away at your personality. Even now, she's not sure what was her mother and what was Alzheimer's. This disease is such a devious imposter. It comes unannounced, offends loved ones and thinks nothing of picking fights and propelling offspring far from the nest. It's robbed Sophie of her mother but also of the memory of her, leaving instead this lingering unease and she's wrapped up in it with her. She needs to grieve, but when? And how far should she travel back in time in order to remember the real person at the centre of her grief?

Her first thought though, when she gets her own result, is that it's funny. She's noticed this in herself before, this gallows humour. Here's a shockingly terrible finding – one that even the doctor wasn't expecting – and she finds it hilarious. She has to be careful now not to show this instant response; it does seem a little deranged and there's probably a ward somewhere near here that isn't so easy to leave. What comes next is hardly better – she feels a massive sense of release. She won't have to worry about pensions or old age or anything long term. She can do whatever she likes, write what she wants, go wherever takes her fancy. They should have a family holiday in…where would be a fantastic place to take the kids, maybe for one last adventure with their mum? In this moment, she feels more alive than ever. The world is full of possibilities.

She doesn't start to take in the reality of it all until she next visits her mother a couple of days later. On the drive up the M6, she has pins and needles in her head, and she's convinced she can feel her brain shrinking. At times it feels as though there's an ice-cold vice across her temple. It's only two days since she picked up the result, but the scan was taken over a year ago, so this must be entirely psychosomatic. She knows this but it still feels real. She imagines that by now there's probably only a tiny walnut left, rattling inside her skull.

Her mother is asleep when she arrives and barely acknowledges her presence when she wakes. She's doubly incontinent and has lost a few front teeth since Sophie last saw her, though no one knows how. There's nothing funny or liberating about her life sentence now.

Instinctively, she wants to distance herself. They're still too tied up and she's in danger of being dragged down with her.

Sorry, Mum. Much though I love you, I don't want to follow you in this one.

The scientist in her is still sceptical. So they have this scan and it's used for early diagnosis of Alzheimer's, but has anyone checked how many normal people are wandering round with under-functioning parietal lobes? She emails the consultant. Yes, it's possible that there are normal people with under-functioning parietal lobes. Oh good, she thinks, but then she remembers that's the point – it's used in early detection – so all those people might be ticking time bombs. She immerses herself in the literature.

Neurodegeneration begins twenty to thirty years before clinical manifestation. This is in line with their experience. But aren't neurons always degenerating? she hears herself plead. And isn't the brain amazing in its plasticity? Aren't there countless examples of the brain compensating for damage by recruiting other areas to take over, and can't neurons proliferate as well as die? Anyway, are those nerves in her brain even dead or just not metabolizing? Is it reversible? She asks the consultant.

'It simply isn't known', he replies.

More rifling through the academic press. It's so infinitely preferable to examining her life right now. Further scans that she doesn't care to think about may have confirmed that she has the disease, but what do doctors know? She bristles at the memory of that arrogant young man telling her to consider cutting down on work and appointing someone to manage her financial affairs. In her mind's eye, his face has taken on something cynical and unscrupulous.

Time passes and nothing changes. Meals cook themselves and she does her share of the work. Then she helps only with the washing up. Then only tidying away the cutlery. This is normal, that kids help more as they get older. She's fine. More than that, she's positively buoyed by the bustle and banter, the music mysteriously emanating from wireless speakers, the toing and froing of boyfriends and girlfriends.

And now there's a pandemic. What a reprieve! A much-dreaded discussion with her boss is put on hold and she continues to work, holding any undesirable feedback at bay by simply closing her laptop. No more awkward interactions. No more unfair advantage as others remember previous encounters, or worse, the niggling suspicion that events are being fabricated – that she's being gaslighted again.

Just the children, sent home from their various places of study.

The world has reopened, and Sophie finds herself in the reception area without an appointment letter. What brought her here?

Her youngest son set up her phone so that she can bark 'take me to . . .' commands at it. Following these simple instructions brought her here, to the front door of this hospital. But why? She looks around for clues. In the large open space where there was once a piano, there's now just emptiness. Dog-eared 'stay 2m apart' stickers cling to the floor, and the way up is barred. What is she doing here? She tries to remember where she was when she set off on her quest, but how do you try to remember? She can barely hold onto a thought, let alone extract more information from somewhere within her mind. Had she been to her son's school? Did he have an important test today, or was she the one being assessed? Did she go in to sit the exam? She sees herself sobbing quietly in the school office and someone consoling her. Did a kindly teacher escort her off the premises? The line between memory and imagination is so tenuous, you can almost decide yourself where to draw it.

'Fuck,' she thinks. She might have said it. The outbursts and muttering that used to so annoy and embarrass her children, nowadays seem to evoke only sadness.

A uniformed man approaches her as she stands in front of a sign – a black exclamation mark on a yellow background.

'You look lost. Can I help?'

'I'm trying to get to neuro ...' the word escapes her.

'Neurology? That's up on the first floor. The escalators are closed for maintenance at the moment. You can take the lift to the first floor, but I think neurology's only Tuesdays and Fridays.'

He presses a button and metal doors open revealing a mirror-lined hole in the wall. She's dimly aware of her mother in the reflection, which confuses her.

Dreamlike sequences with ill-defined aims and nebulous characters are punctured by moments of intense clarity, with all her emotions heightened. She even feels something of what others feel, like this woman at reception.

'Doctor Digby doesn't work on Mondays,' she says, with a look of disdain. 'Today's ophthalmology.'

Her scowl and tight lips conjure up Sophie's ex. Sophie knows she's the cause of this irritation; the fierce distaste flared up in response to Sophie's presence, but what has she done? How does she elicit such hatred? There's no mileage in any further interaction and she feels herself siding with her critics.

'Fucker,' she says to herself, maybe out loud.

Eventually she's escorted down a corridor, through a courtyard, to an entrance that states 'Mental Health Unit'. Earlier, someone had gently prised the phone from her hand and called her emergency contact number and now she's waiting here.

'Your friend will be here soon,' she's told.

She sits in an armchair, reliving snippets of dreams and memories. She's lecturing, wrapped in a towel which slips off. There's a burglary. She enters the house and that same instant, intruders snatch her children, and she knows she'll never see them again. A wad of something pungent is being held over her face and she can't move, and somewhere she knows she's partially to blame. She should have done it all differently.

She roots around in her mind to conjure up a positive memory and settles on the look of pride her mother gave her whenever she jumped through some carefully placed maths hoop. Then the symbols and numbers themselves appear. They'd stood in as such benevolent proxies throughout her childhood. She closes her eyes and watches her old friends – ε γ φ and π – as each acquires a life of its own. It's quite extraordinary, the way they're dancing.

Someone is stroking her hand, and a familiar voice says: 'You looked so peaceful I didn't want to wake you. You were smiling in your sleep.' A woman in a grey linen dress wraps her arms around her.

'Come on,' she says, as though a special bond exists between them. 'Let's go home.'

///checklist.combative.frontman
by Conor McAnally

I stand in shattered silence as the groans begin to grow, the aftermath of ball bearing and bomb bedlam. Shards of skin and lifeless limb lie everywhere around. The screams surround from gaping mouths but are muted now in my blocked ears. I've been deafened by the blast but am otherwise unscathed. A miracle, I think. Beside me lie the ripped remains of friends and other travelers. Who will say a prayer for them? Hold the guilty to account? I look around the fallen room for an answer and it comes. Someone who has skills and time to investigate, identify and track, to hunt until the bloody end, wherever that may be. And I know that person must be me.

I bind the wounds, close some eyes and hold a hand or two until the dark smoke is penetrated by flashing red and blue. Paramedics rush to triage and I help as best I can, pointing to the suffering, indicating those who've gone, standing back, allowing room and stumbling away, scared where I place my feet lest I stand on pieces of a friend. Back against a wall I slump, shock draining my resources, no strength in legs, my flapping arms try to wave away the scene, but I stare at every gurney, every body bag and first responder. They're here now, picking carefully through the blasted debris, helping with the bodies until they point to me. I am almost invisible propped against this wall. The clouds of gray concrete dust have mono-chromed us all.

'Are you alright sir?' they say in voices that are audible but very far away. 'Sir, sir,' they repeat, 'are you injured?'

I cannot answer, I don't know. I feel nothing in my body. Only devastation in my soul.

'Can you move?' they ask, and I nod my head in hope, try to rise but fail and hit the floor. Pathetic lack of resolve, I think. Stand up, you bastard. I try and fail again, shake my head in resignation. What has happened to my voice? Why do I have no tongue? Is this the sum of carnaged horror, being struck deaf and dumb? A constable squats beside me. The other officers move on. Then she beckons to a paramedic, someone else for me to cling onto, hoping his face might reassure. The examination is meticulous, fingertip to toe, pressing here, poking there, careful to explore all of my exposed body. There, below my heart, he discovers a small puncture mark, a hole that leaks darkened blood quietly into the cloth, something I've been unaware of until his gentle probe. Now I'm jolting forward and have found my voice. Phlegm, dust, and disgust shoot out of my mouth. And the pain-pierced sound grows animal as my angered horror growls.

They have me on a gurney, cutting off my clothes, searching for the blood hole to stem the flow and, in doing so, discover more. Multiple perforations. They prepare for operation. My scream has cleared my ears but what I hear concerns. It's all numbers and acronyms they explain in childlike terms, not that I understand, and when the needle pricks, I start to drift and leave it all behind. The slide to darkness is pleasant. I'm happy to depart.

I wake anesthetized, pain free, stitched inside and out, devoid of metal. The ball bearings are on a tray beside me. Standard IED material. A cool hand touches my arm and I turn, furry-mouthed, to say, 'Hey,' or something that sounds similar. The hand gestures at the metal dish.

'Have you seen what you wished?'

Her accent seems familiar but I can't reach it.

'Wished?'

'Oh yes, you insisted.'

I've lost part of my liver and something nicked my spleen, a punctured lung and abdomen, but otherwise I'm free of life-threatening injury, but I will not be discharged.

'What about my head?'

'No trauma, it's superficial.'

Cuts and nicks, I think, probably quite trivial, but the mirror in the bathroom tells a different story. The face that stares back at me is pretty bloody gory. The swollen nose and slitted eyes, pock-marked skin dark-stained with dust are all too damn familiar. I've seen that picture much too often in places like Fallujah.

I discharge myself against the medical advice. I nod my head in acquiescence at the discharge instructions — rest and recuperation, a slow build back to normal — in one ringing ear and out the other. I stop the taxi at a phone shop and buy myself some burners. What comes next will be off the grid and I must protect the unit. No eavesdroppers on this solo mission as I hunt down the bombers and deliver retribution. I text Frankie from the flat. Burner numbers out of sequence. No problem, since he knows my code.

Deriinng, deriing, the old Bakelite ringtone.

'Wotcha mate, you understand why... — ' he says.

'Yeah, of course, you couldn't. Security. You busy?'

'Intelligence is on it. Bravo standing by.'

'What's the chatter?'

'Remember Isis Charlie?' he whispers.

'We missed him, got his brother.'

'They reckon he's behind it, although at this stage no one's certain.'

'Enough for me.'

'You're not thinking — wait, have you reported in?'

'Presumed sick leave, mate. You know the drill.'

Frankie starts to protest, so I disconnect the call. Better he knows nothing. Not yet. Maybe not at all.

Money is a war weapon and Americans always have more than anyone. They fly it into combat zones on pallets, shrink-wrapped new dollars by the millions. Because they have so much, they don't properly keep track. It's easy to get a little in your back pocket. Money for bribes and compensation, blood money for shootings — meant or accidental — cash for crimes committed on a population, dollars for intelligence and useful information. I repeat back to them what they first told me. They hand me wads of currency and call it confirmation.

Here in my anonymous lock-up, I open an ammo case stuffed with dollars from their intelligence agencies. In between the acronyms, the money flows quite freely. Give a fighter enough cash — he might not be your enemy. Around me in the lamplit space are all my other trophies, weapon systems I've acquired on deniable covert missions. They took the dark route home concealed in military transportation.

There's a dealer that I know sells vans below a railway bridge in Acton. Ted is not a curious bloke. He takes it all in slow and smiles a hefty price at you — part remuneration, part lack of speculation. What you do is up to you once he's got his wages. I drive the anonymous white van back to the anonymous gray storage unit and load up out of camera view with green and khaki boxes.

Ferry boats are convenient but traceable. Customs and security everywhere, thanks to bloody Brexit. But there are other routes abroad, quieter ways to cross the sea. My van is in a container heading for Zeebrugge.

I travel separately by ferry and train, cash in hand, no credit card trail. A large floppy hat casts shadows deep across my face and I walk, head down, with an unhurried pace, past cameras in terminals, stations and streets. Nothing to see here, nothing out of place. It's hard to find something if you're not even looking. And they aren't. Yet. I get to the warehouse in Holland, unload the container and drive into Europe. The painkillers don't work so well. My stomach hurts and starts to swell. I drive with ice packs round my middle. It helps a little.

You make partial friends in this kind of game. Our languages are different but experiences the same. We train together in desert and ice, jungle, ocean, air and mountain. We splice parts of our lives in trust of each other. A warrior's bond. Real blood brothers.

GSG9 Freddie has things that I need, a pickup in Munich and a debt partly repaid. Jean Pierre from Le Commando Hubert books passage for me from Marseilles across the Mediterranean Sea. The dragnet is closing on Isis Charlie's team and location. Location is the key. That's where his final reckoning will be. Charlie will be cautious and on edge, aware that somewhere plans are being made, intelligence gathered, a strike force assembled. He'll move to one of his strongholds, double security, looking for signs of a raid—but not for me.

Being really ordinary is the best part of deception. There's nothing about me to draw attention. Average height and build, wiry but not muscled, hair brown and no military cut, clothes dull and unremarkable. No strong color to catch an eye. No strange behavior to remember me by. I am nobody among everybody, slipping through the miles unseen.

There's blood in my urine.

I make another call to Frankie, who's concerned. Wants to know where I am. The regiment's aware now of my absence.

'The Colonel wants to see you,' Frankie says.

'And he will, but first I have some biz. Is Charlie where I might expect to find him?'

'You know I can't give intel.'

'Can you help a mate?'

In the silence, I sense his debate and finally he says, 'I can't tell you anything, but with your nose you should find him by the smell.'

I smile and cut the line. Saying more would compromise, and Frankie is a friend.

There's a town in Syria where sulfur spoils the air. Now they process natural gas there. On the outskirts, there's a compound I saw once on satellite imagery. That's where Isis Charlie will be.

I swap my Volkswagen Transporter for a Hyundai van in Turkey. The VW would stand out like a beacon. Yusuf from Turk Maroon Berets gladly lets me know the score on the border crossing, where the checkpoints are, who's in control. I'm more confident now and anyway, I've been down these roads before. Enough said.

Finally, I'm near. I trawl the town in thobe and Arab headgear, looking for a space to set my base. After two days, I find it and hike back to the desert to retrieve the van. In the gathering dusk, I drive into the crumbling husk of a once beautiful villa. No prying eye from street or sky can see the Hyundai.

With a base set, I begin to scout for an observation post. Charlie's compound is well guarded and the sentries seem on point. There's a cluster of flat-topped buildings not too far away. With night vision, I scale one and slide silently in place with MRE's and water sufficient for a week. It takes three days, but I get my confirmation. Charlie's there with all his team. There's no time for hesitation. I've picked my vantage point, seen their sentry changes, studied their routes and found some empty spaces where I can crawl into my hide. Ideally, I would like more time but have to stay flexible. I have no way of knowing Isis Charlie's schedule.

Nightly, I prepare the killing ground. Claymore mines are an infiltrator's most reliable friend. Seven hundred metal balls traveling at velocity will take out anyone in a hundred-yard vicinity. An eye for an eye, a ball for a ball. With my blood and leaking body fluids, I know that it is fitting.

Before dawn, as I climb the outside wall, I feel one lung collapse. A stiletto through my shoulder blade and vice around my rib cage. But I have no time for this and snake up to my sniper's nest. Underneath my khaki ghillie suit, I should be pretty much invisible. The HK417 lies against my good shoulder, scope calibrated, twenty rounds in the magazine. Tonight is when the bullets fly, when I begin the mayhem. I need the dark. It's part of my escape plan. And just then Charlie appears, unmistakable in the harsh sunlight, and walks towards a vehicle. I'm incredulous, but seeing is believing. Charlie and his terror team are leaving.

I snick a round into the chamber and fire between my breaths. His head explodes, down he goes. His terror's done forever. The rest scatter, firing in all directions, searching for my location. I pick them off, one by one, but there are so many. A bead of sweat forms above my eye and this thought occurs. What is revenge and who does it serve? Is it worth the jangling nerves that twitch around my eyeball and make the guarantee of accuracy uncertain? What is justice and accountability, what is redress and responsibility, where is karma in this scheme? What do any of these words mean when bullets tear through fragile flesh and blood spurts red and fresh, staining face and shoes and shirt, splattering on walls and earth? Who is terrorist now — the bomber, or the triggered round, the revenger or the fallen?

Why do I pursue this path? For others or for myself? Am I an avenging angel or simply death itself? I could speak to the bodies I helped bury, caskets borne on hardened shoulder and harder soul. Would their voices call me to this slaughter, or sing a different song about right and two wrongs? A part of me is anxious, wanting to know the reason for my presence. Am I here for king and country or for my own vainglory? Is it just because I have nowhere else to be? No wife, no kids, no family. I'm the last of the line and maybe that is good. All of my forefathers have been bathed in blood. A century of service to soldiering, marching and maneuvering. Charging, maiming, killing in service of an empire expanding. Like a virus.

I fire all twenty of my rounds and change the magazine, but they keep spilling from the buildings. Angry, like hornets spitting flame. I depended on the darkness, but this is light of day. The escape route depended on Plan A. I wish I had Plan B.

Who will say a prayer for me? Hold the guilty to account? I look around the dead-bodied square and the charging fedayeen. The Claymores were a last resort to cover my escape, but I'm still on the wall — well within the kill zone. They advance on my sniper mount, AKs at the ready. I breathe. My hands are steady.

I will say a prayer for me. Hold the guilty to account. I mouth my hymn, say hello to Him and press the detonator.

///lobby.froze.surveyed
by Nina Smith

Cee's biggest downfall was that she was likeable. It wasn't a bad trait, not by any stretch. Her affable nature had taken her far. Class President at school, head of several clubs at college, and it had undoubtedly fast-tracked her career at one of the world's biggest law firms. But, what she failed to recognise was the difference between being likeable and needing to be liked. A subtle distinction she did not yet understand. She was so *nice* in fact, that when she walked in on a colleague and found him slumped over his desk, dead as discarded roadkill, her first instinct had been to apologise. Saying sorry was a terrible habit of hers.

Cee was deeply aware of her niceness. And she knew that as much as it propelled her forward, it also held her back. She'd been presented with the evidence many times over the years – romantic acquaintances seamlessly ghosting their way out of her life without being held to account; people asking favours they'd *never* consider asking anyone else (always knowing the answer would, of course, be an obliging and enthusiastic yes); and most recently, most irrefutably, being sent to Tokyo on secondment rather than being given the promotion that had so clearly belonged to her.

'I'm sorry,' she'd said after a silence lingered uncomfortably in the air as she tried to compute how she could have been overlooked for the role.

Her boss, Miles Franklin, was a pock-marked man with a long track-record of bringing in lucrative clients to the firm and a propensity for complaining about 'political correctness gone mad' when topics such as diversity or parental leave were brought up. He had broken the news to her from his desk in London as she stood, on the other side, stunned, racking her mind for what she possibly could have done (or not done) to warrant this gut-wrenching oversight.

'It'll be an adventure for you,' he'd said. 'If you can prove yourself with one more client, then we can reconsider. You're not the only one vying for this role, after all.'

Cee wanted to scream at him, upend his desk, and howl like a rabid dog for the loss of something she'd worked years for. She wanted to tell him that she was aware that she wasn't the only one vying for the role, while reminding him that she was the only one who was actually viable for the role.

Instead, she'd said, 'Tokyo, of course, yes,' while walking backwards out of his office. She couldn't remember for certain, but half recollected thanking him on her way out. *For what?*

Of course, she would never cause a scene. *Nice* women don't kick up a fuss.

Cee reflected on this conversation as she wove through the sea of desks, her intrusive thoughts tuning out the thrumming of fingers across keyboards, reams of paper being spewed out from printers and fax machines, and the low drum of office chatter that sounded like white noise because she understood only a handful of Japanese phrases. She could have just said *no*. She could have pushed back, demanding she be given the promotion that she deserved. She could have quit. Yet, here she was. In Tokyo, a vibrating metropolis that under any other circumstance would have been a destination she'd love to visit if she ever allowed herself to take time off work.

'You can't let yourself be overlooked,' Theo had told her over a bowl of ramen in an *izakaya* last night. Cee had grown to love the ramshackle hole-in-the-wall style eateries that were tucked away in small laneways and underneath train station arches that ran like veins through the network of tightly packed concrete and steel monoliths making up Tokyo. They pulsed with life and colour, and salarymen loosening their collars after long days bent over unforgiving desks. Smoke billowed out from the open coal fires as shots of *saké* and *shōchū* were consumed in all directions. Whether it was some magical ingredient in the healing broth of the ramen, or the wizened, kind eyes of the man tending to his *yakitori* behind the very same grill he'd been manning for decades, she felt as though those evenings injected life back into her.

'Every office is full of mediocre people amplifying their lukewarm achievements,' Theo said, slurping a hand-rolled noodle through his lips. 'Your excellence speaks for itself.'

'Exactly,' Cee responded, her steaming broth splashing over the sides of the bowl as her noodles slipped from her chopsticks. 'Why can't Miles see that? Why don't the partners see that?'

'Because that's not how it works in the corporate world. You've got to be your own one-man PR team.'

'That's easy for you to say, you *are* a one-man PR team.'

Theo was a public relations whizz who acted almost exclusively for Abe & Wright, muffling their PR fires and publicising their successes on a global scale. She saw him regularly when she was back home in London, where he was also based, but had caught up with him the handful of times he'd flown out to the Tokyo office during her stint. As a consultant ('I refuse to become a corporate slave beholden to one master,' he'd always say), he was both part of the firm and far removed from it, so had a distant yet magnified appreciation of the firm's political landscape.

'Call it what you like. PR, spin. Everyone does it,' he said, with the authority of someone who lived and breathed their chosen profession. 'The art of self-promotion is key. Simply doing the good work is not enough. If a tree falls in an empty forest, and all that.'

'Yeah, yeah, I get it.' Cee said, wanting to move the conversation on. She had no problem waxing lyrical about the world-class expertise of the legal teams she put forward in her tenders or at meetings with prospective clients, but the thought of promoting her own work felt uncomfortably foreign to her. It wasn't entirely lost on her that not doing so had landed her in an actual foreign land.

Theo picked up the menu again, a laminated sheet of paper, sides curled and tattered.

'I worry about you,' he said, not taking his eyes from the menu. She could see them darting across the columns listing the various foods on offer. Each item was described in both Japanese and English, though many of the letters had long been eroded from the page. 'You need to avoid *karoshi*.'

'*Karoshi*?' Cee said, leaning in to look at the same columns. 'I don't see that on the menu.'

'Seriously, Cee, learn some Japanese already.' Theo said, rolling his eyes in patient amusement. '*Karoshi* means death from overwork.'

'That's a Japanese thing?'

'It's an everywhere thing. They just have a word for it here. Look, all I'm saying is don't kill yourself working for a firm that would replace you in a heartbeat.'

'A heartbeat?'

'Someone else's heartbeat,' he said, and then pointed his chopsticks squarely at Cee's chest. 'Not yours.'

Now, as Cee approached Hiroshi Tanaka's office for their scheduled meeting, she froze, only briefly, and inhaled the custom fragrance that was piped throughout the law firm's lobby and corridors. It was an innocuous blend of Hinoki cypress and English oak, which teetered between subtle nod to the firm's British-Japanese heritage and odorous marketing gimmick. His door was closed but she could see his outline through the frosted glass panel next to it, unmoving in concentration.

Hiroshi Tanaka was the lead partner of the mergers and acquisitions group based in Tokyo, the most profitable team of Abe & Wright globally. She hadn't managed to make much of an impression on him since she'd arrived two months ago, partly because of his reticence to accept her expertise (when visiting London, he frequented the same members-only venue, a literal old boys' club, as Miles did), and also because there hadn't been the right opportunity. But now was the moment. It *had* to be the moment. Hiroshi Tanaka was a close friend of her boss, and though there was an ocean, several land masses and innumerable cultural differences between them, it was impossible to overestimate the influence that Hiroshi Tanaka had on Miles Franklin. On everyone, for that matter. This news would seal the deal. It had to.

She knocked on the door of his office, the most prestigious of the forty-five window-facing offices reserved solely for the more senior partners of the firm. Along one wall were bookshelves lined with legal tomes and various industry awards accrued over decades spent working on some of the world's most notable transactions. Several framed photos punctuated the shelves, but rather than images of family, they displayed photos of him meeting other suited men. Cee didn't recognise any of them, but they all looked important somehow. Heads of industry, government leaders, that kind of thing. His desk was expansive, a solid cherrywood block that seemingly floated across the middle of the room, centred by a high-backed leather chair with a worn-in grosgrain patina that arose from great expense rather than the passage of time. Hiroshi Tanaka was a *deals man*, and his office was almost as intimidating as he was. But what really stood this room apart was the view, the floor-to-ceiling window perfectly framing the gardens of Tokyo's Imperial Palace that spread out beyond it. It was as if the building existed first, and the centuries-old gardens were formed solely for this window. A lush lung in the middle of one of the City's numerous business districts, all monolithic steel skyscrapers, treelined yet grey pavements, and suited workers scurrying about their business in homogenous harried urgency. Despite herself, Cee found the gardens enchanting, and often strolled into them during her lunch breaks, captivated by the sheer magnitude of the pristine botanical perfection.

'Excuse me, Mr Tanaka,' she said. The door was ajar, so she took a tentative step inside, and let out a courtesy cough. 'I'm here for our meeting.'

She was there to break good news about the major client win she'd secured for the firm. Or was it only bad news that was broken? The opposite of breaking something is fixing it, and she thought this news had that quality. Like the Japanese art of *kintsugi*, where gold is painted over the cracks of shattered pottery to fuse it back into one piece, rendered more beautiful by its imperfection. She hoped that was what this news would be, the liquid gold fusing together the broken pieces that made up her career and everything she'd sacrificed for it. Miles had more or less assured the promotion was hers if she could pull this off. And she had pulled this off.

She wanted to be the first to tell Hiroshi Tanaka. Her experience had taught her that news of this sort, of work yielding victorious results, was often accredited more favourably to the messenger than to the person who did the actual work, like the antithesis to shooting the messenger. This was certainly the case with Zachary Thompson. Zachary, whose golf handicap was on par with his ability to deliver the most well-timed compliment. Zachary, a master at delegating while glossing over the smaller details, knowing someone else would take care of them (and that someone was, almost always, Cee). Zachary, who sat in London, pawing at *her* role. He had the uncanny ability to insert himself into Cee's orbit, absorbing her efforts and contribution into his own. She'd never spoken up about it. *Nice* women don't complain about that kind of thing.

She took another step towards Hiroshi Tanaka's desk and blurted out the news before he had a chance to acknowledge her presence. She knew she should revel in the delivery, but she was desperate to get it off her chest, this million-dollar news that would somehow righten the trajectory of her career, and her life. She'd poured hours upon hours into winning over this client, and many others throughout the years, regularly declining invitations to social events, or accepting invitations and then not turning up, until those invitations eventually petered out. The only friends she caught up with regularly now were Theo and a few others from the office. She had given her life to Abe & Wright, and now, it had all culminated in this win. This win belonged to the firm, to the team. But also, it belonged to *her*. Miles had been quite clear that whoever won this client would secure that promotion. And Zachary was 6,000 miles away so couldn't take an iota of credit that wasn't his. Not this time.

It was Cee's absorption in these details that meant it took her longer than it should have to survey the details in front of her. Hiroshi Tanaka's chair was positioned in the exact middle of the desk, in a precise symmetry that reflected the gardens behind him. Her eyes went immediately to the view, it always did, but then they landed on the desk and a box of expensive Japanese whiskey adorned with a gold bow holding in place a little notecard. The bottle had been removed from the carton, and the top lay next to an Abe & Wright-branded glass that held a finger of the amber liquid. Her eyes flicked back to the notecard. It was white and embossed with the sender's initials on the front. She squinted to read it. At first it reminded her of the mark of Zorro, and she almost laughed, until she realised the Z did not stand for the caped crusader.

'No!' Cee gasped, unsure if she did so out loud or in her head.

She looked at Hiroshi Tanaka's eyes, hoping he'd confirm in a surprised glance that Zachary hadn't pulled off what she'd thought was impossible. Not again, surely. Perhaps the card was unrelated. Perhaps it wasn't even from Zachary.

It was then she noticed that the most powerful man in the office hadn't acknowledged her. In fact, he hadn't even moved.

There was something grisly about the way he sat, so still, his arm outstretched across the table, his laptop pushed aside, and his hand gnarled around his mouse. He was slumped sideways in a way that looked jarring rather than slovenly. His jaw hung slack yet rigid, and his eyes. Oh, his eyes. Not closed nor open, they bore a haunted cast she'd never seen before but would from that point recognise as the telling sign of a life departed.

The air felt thick, like the humidity from beyond the glass windows had penetrated through the windows. The office scent disappeared, replaced by a foreign smell that unsettled something deep inside her.

A tumult of panic swirled in Cee's gut, and she felt the blast of the air-conditioning vents bleat icy daggers onto the back of her neck. She dropped the papers she was holding and brought her hands to her neck. The client win, the win that meant everything, plummeted out of her mind.

'Oh no, Mr Tanaka,' she said. Her face burnt with an awkward cocktail of embarrassment and fear, and she stumbled backward a few steps. 'I'm so sorry. You're dead.'

///with.with.space
by Ben Tufnell

Dear Sir,

I believe that you will find the enclosed document of interest. It is a transcription of a handwritten note recovered from an abandoned building in south London. It had been uninhabited for many years and was scheduled for demolition.

A large Victorian structure, originally constructed as a private hospital, it had been converted into apartments at some point in the early twentieth century. Long empty, for the last decade it stood isolated in the centre of a run-down area waiting to be cleared to make way for a new development of luxury apartments. As you may know, this area has been much gentrified in recent years. We were engaged to affect the clearance.

Interestingly, in our dealings with the local community we learnt that the old building was known (ironically) as 'The Palace'. It was rumoured to be used as a meeting place for druggists, deviants and political agitators. As a matter of course, children were warned by their parents to avoid going anywhere near it, especially after nightfall.

The papers in question were found in empty rooms on the third floor, in what was once one of the largest apartments. It had evidently been uninhabited for many years but still held the detritus of the last occupant. The ruins of the glass construction mentioned in the text were in the largest room. We found no trace of the author or, indeed, of the inhabitants of said glass structure.

Many hundreds of books, which must once have constituted an extensive library, had long since succumbed to damp and mould. In the drawers of a writing desk were piles of decaying papers. These few pages were the only legible items. They were written in a beautiful cursive script. On reading them I was struck by the unusual contents and, as they were so fragile, I immediately made a copy.

The building and its contents are now gone. Work has just begun on the new development.

What do you make of it?

Yours etc.

On waking, I don't know if it is day or night; there is no way of telling. God only knows how long I have been like this, on the floor with my head against the stone-cold radiator. An hour? A day? A month?

In considerable pain, I turn on the lights but they hurt my eyes and so I turn them off again and light a candle instead. As always, it is hard to tell if I am really awake, or if this is yet another bad dream. The ache in my frontal lobe tells me it is the former. Looking down at myself, pale and painted with orange shapes by the flickering candlelight, I can see that there is hardly anything left.

In the kitchen, the taps are dry and dusty. Many webs. I drink old water from a filthy glass. In the refrigerator the milk has long gone over and become a sickly yellow solid. There are other things in there that defy identification. The room stinks of death and I can hear the rats playing in the cupboards, as if to taunt me. Voices come to me, faint and unintelligible, something like the soft white noise of static, but it might just be the wind in the chimneys. I wander through the rooms and down the passageways disturbing the dust into satisfying clouds, mobile diagrams of entropy. As always, the mice and rats ignore me and continue their feverish activity, gnawing and scurrying. In the drawing room I locate a glass and pour myself port. Carrying it through into the sitting room, I step carefully over the piles of books. Settling into an armchair, I watch the television, which is badly tuned. Through all the interference I can just about make out a commentary on the war. But it does not interest me.

[*This concludes the first part of the text, which continues on a separate sheet*]

I no longer have any doubts that I will die here. Perhaps even here at this very desk. I cannot remember the last time I went outside, at least not with any certainty. Sometimes I pull back the heavy curtains and see the cars rushing past and the rain pouring from the dreary sky and that is enough. In fact, it is too much. Then I return to the darkness, and perhaps listen to the last of the records that have not been ruined by careless scratching and chewing of the abominable rodents.

Thankfully, it is no longer necessary to see or interact with anyone. Due to my careful preparation for this phase, every month a food parcel is deposited upon the landing outside my door. There used to be mail from time to time but that stopped coming long ago. Yes, I am isolated here, and it is as it should be. I need solitude to prepare for the next step.

This place was built as an asylum, and I fancy sometimes that some psychic echo of the poor souls who once suffered beneath this roof still remains. They float from room to room like scraps of mist, searching always for something that is no longer here. No one occupies the apartment above anymore and I sometimes creep up there at night and sit under the skylight, observing the phases of the moon. I believe an old man and a cat live below me. I have never seen him, but I once heard him shouting at the wretched creature, cursing it. Sometimes it ascends the stairs and scratches at my front door, perhaps sensing the rodents, but when I open it to see, it flees. But now that I think of it, it seems to me that I have not heard his shufflings and clangings for some time, and the diabolical beast has not scraped at the door for an age. There is only silence. And the strangely musical whisperings of the wind in the chimneys.

Alas, thick dust and cobwebs are everywhere. In places the carpets are white with the particles of plaster that fall like pollen from the decaying ceiling roses. I must admit that things have gone too far now, have gotten out of hand. I have let it happen. But there is no going back. I don't have the strength to tidy anymore. Even writing is a struggle. It is as much as I can do now to take a tin of soup down from one of the cupboards and gently warm it on the hob.

My beloved books, unopened for years (for my eyesight is failing) are stacked all about in disarray (where once they were meticulously ordered and indexed) and are being slowly destroyed by the damp. It is a tragedy. They fester in corners and lie upon the shelves like corpses. The opulence of this apartment, once so grand, which took me so much time and money to achieve, has long been replaced by the rank air of a mausoleum. And yet still I dare not open the windows. I look up at the walls and the buckling and warping of the canvasses make the portraits of my ancestors seem like ghouls leering at me terribly, but I do not flinch under their accusing gazes.

[*Here several passages in the original manuscript are illegible due to heavy staining*]

I wake to find the glass of port has slipped from my feeble grasp and fallen to the floor. What looks like a bloodstain spreads slowly through the ragged pile of the carpet and a black rat the size of a cat licks greedily at it. I try to kick it, but it ignores me. I stare at it, powerless. Eventually it loses interest and wobbles lazily from my sight. I lose interest too, get up and wander painfully back through my rooms to the rancid kitchen where I warm a tin of watery soup and drink it slowly from the pan and feel a little of my strength returning.

[*The paper has rotted and come apart here*]

Aside from the rodents, the only sign of life is in the bedchamber. This is where the Palace is. It takes up almost half the room; a glittering construction of glass and metal lit by bluish strip lights. My design. My treasure. This is the thing that keeps me going. It is here that the Bugs live.

An ingenious system of pumps and filters and heaters keep the Palace supplied with everything they need; it nourishes the plants they depend on. Luxuriant ferns press against the glass and exotic flowers strain towards the lights. When they burst into bloom, as they occasionally do, it is as if the brightly coloured *coronae* of veiny purples and bloody reds illuminate the entire room, refracted through the crystal prisms of the Palace walls.

And while the plants flourish, so too do the Bugs. Where once there were only two, obtained at great expense and with devious negotiation, there are now eleven. Eleven! Just three or four inches long, their hard black shells, shining with the iridescence of petrol, are shaped like bullets. They wear on them indecipherable hieroglyphs of luminous lapis blue. In the Palace they live a slow and somnolent life, as I do, often not moving for many days, occasionally rousing themselves to chew absently on a leaf or flower or to lay the eggs. They are the only thing that keeps me going. Many times, I have found myself seated on a chair facing the Palace, staring at one of the strange creatures, following it with my bug eyes as it makes its way up the stem of a plant, transfixed by the purity of *the idea*.

Entering the bedchamber, I set down the candle and contemplate the glassy construction. After a while I bring my face up against the glass and feel its warmth against my skin. It is really very beautiful. I can see one of the holy beasts, its carapace seemingly glowing from within, making a slow journey from one side of the Palace to the other. A cluster of eggs hangs beneath a leaf on one of the largest of the ferns. I cannot help but rub my hands together in a childish gesture of happiness. There are six, each a creamy yellow and about the size of a marble. Perfection. As always, they remind me of the milky eyes of a blind child, staring at me in the blue light. The paradox is that they confer sight.

Carefully, I reach in and pull them free. Five is the most I have dared to take before. These ones are new, moist and warm but firm to the touch. I look at them closely: not strictly speaking eggs, but egg-sacs. One by one I put them in my mouth (they have an oily texture) and swallow them down with a gulp of port. There is an aftertaste, sour and bitter, that mingles with the alcohol in an unpleasant way.

There is no sound but for the dripping of water in one of the filters. As I close my eyes, I hear someone calling my name from a very great distance. It can only be the wind in the chimneys.

[*Here the original manuscript has apparently been gnawed at by rodents. Some text is lost.*]

When I eat the eggs and their mysteries have passed into my bloodstream, a great coolness fills me. Sometimes I sit and stare at the slow movement of the clock (I have, on occasion, watched the hands go all the way around, never once taking my eyes off them). Under the influence, time has a different quality.

My thoughts feel like solid objects, turning and tumbling in a great void. I close my eyes and see fabulous visions, alien worlds lit with strange clarity, pulsing fairground landscapes, great crystal cities, vast deserts and jewelled forests. Long ago, I became convinced that these visions are of real places, not some form of interior mental projection or imaginative construction.

With time, I am learning to control these visions.

I have become aware that with increased dosage my immersion in this other dimension is more complete. I now believe that with a strong enough hit it will be possible to cross a threshold, to leave this defunct universe and enter the other one, which is brighter. Psychotropic transubstantiation, I suppose one might call it. Our star is dying, and soon all will be dark. But upon the other side, the sun still burns strongly.

It has not happened yet, although I feel I come closer with every attempt. The eggs are escape vehicles.

Whether a return will be possible, I cannot say.

I can feel it beginning.

I will leave the beautiful blue lights (so like the interior of a glacier) and replenish my glass from the decanter in the drawing room. My favourite armchair awaits me before the empty grate in the cold black fireplace.

I will finish these notes, extinguish the candle, sit down and wait for it to happen.

[*There is no signature*]

///worker.rise.switch
by Sandy Foster

I am stuck at amber. I have been stuck at amber now for longer than is usual, for longer than is normal. When I pulled onto this street, I could see the amber light at the crossroads beaming in the middle distance like a little sun. The cars ahead had already slowed to a stop and I arrived neatly behind, the purr of waiting engines warming the still air.

I checked my watch automatically, though I knew without looking that I'd left the house with plenty of time. I always leave with plenty of time and today's no different. I turned the radio up a little, half listening to the chatter of disembodied voices, wound my window down and up, pushed the air conditioning button on, then off. I adjusted my rear-view mirror, smoothed my hair, checked the glove box for nothing in particular. All to avoid the unbearable stillness threatening to spill into the car.

The moment arrived when one would expect the light to turn green, that buzz of anticipation, a shared sense that we might be about to move. The cars that moments ago were crossing in front of us also now at a stand-still, their own amber holding them in suspension. Engines gently revving in preparation, hands returning mobile phones to bags and pockets, necks craning back as the dregs of coffee are downed. Ready to go. But the moment passed. The lights didn't change. And we are still here.

An impatience with this determined little light is growing. There's an unsettled feeling in the air, like a sound too high for the human ear to hear, raising the heart rate, rattling the bone marrow, sending spiders scurrying across the skin. Two cars back someone beeps their horn, hopeful that the sudden noise might stir the missing green from its slumber, alert it to its tardiness. Perhaps the green will arrive, out of breath, half dressed, apologetically incandescent with colour, Go, *Go*. Perhaps, this amber is in fact the delayed green, face flushed with embarrassment, unrecognisable.

But no. This amber has a confidence. An air of superiority. Of certainty. Confused faces now appear miniatured in rear-view mirrors, headlights flicker on and off absentmindedly. I check my watch again, this time with a nag of anxiety. I glance at the papers on the passenger seat, stacked and stapled, eager to be handed out to bored colleagues. I pick them up, shuffle them, read the first sentence as if taking my eyes from the traffic light for a second might bring about the change more quickly. Watched paint never dries and the same must be true of a traffic light.

As more cars arrive, the pressure behind me begins to build and a few more people join in with the beeping. Some beep lightly, an apologetic question, *is something wrong?* Others beat their steering wheels firmly, sharp loud pips that demand an explanation. One person holds their horn down so there's a long continuous bellow, an attempt at taking the lead, stepping up nose to nose with the offending light. Or perhaps they've collapsed, their dead weight landing heavily onto the steering wheel, and soon the ambulance will arrive, weaving through the traffic, flashing lights screaming impotently. A group of people beep all at once now, a definitive beeping at the beeping, a demand to desist from this futile behaviour. The dead man releases his head from the horn, surrendering. Death isn't ready for him yet. He must wait, like the rest of us.

In spite of this rush of impatience, the amber light remains, firm, resolute, unmoving. The silence that follows the explosion of noise is louder still, alarming in its absoluteness, making human discord look pathetic, inconsequential. Eventually, the man in front opens his car door and throws his legs out, as if the two limbs were all he possessed. *Don't make me come over there,* the legs seem to insist. When this small threat changes nothing, his arms appear and he pushes the whole of him up and out. He looks up at the lights, back at the tailgate. Shrugs.

I should be at work by now, I should be handing out these papers, negotiating with the projector screen, pouring coffee into paper cups. I think about the boardroom, booked ahead by the depressed temp on reception, the flickering strip light no one has thought to fix, the windows that won't open for fear of what people might do.

The amber light persists and the standing man is joined by another. Unlike the first, this second man leaves his car abruptly, an implication he can bear the musty interiors no longer. I watch as he confronts the first man, as if it were he, and not the amber light, that has held us up. They speak low, gesticulating towards the light, looking back across the snake of traffic behind and the cars ahead at the crossroads. I watch as the second man's face flushes, his fists balling up like pickled walnuts. The first man laughs. Guttural. Condescending.

I imagine my colleagues slowly ambling into the board room by now, preparing themselves for another two hours in an airless box to hear talk of deliverables and competencies and blue-sky thinking. The disconcerting mix of BO and air freshener, the muffled *tap, tap, tap,* of keyboards from the adjoining office and the squeak as human bodies negotiate leather wheelie chairs. I should call the office, tell them I'm going to be late, but what can I say, other than *I am stuck at amber*? How can such an incident be explained to those outside of it, if it can be called an incident at all. It would be easier for them to understand the usual excuses: *I ate a bad curry; the boiler burst; my husband has left me and I'm putting my head in the oven.* Those are things people can understand. Things people can comprehend and write down and file away, never to think of again. This is something else.

The second man pushes the first. I don't know why. Perhaps he thinks we should bypass the amber, use our common sense, move forward. After all, there is no traffic coming the other way, no threat of an accident. You too might think this a kind of madness, this indecisiveness, the reluctance for any of us to make the first move. If someone would just ignore the traffic lights and simply move on, we'd all be free from this purgatory. But you're not here. So, you can't possibly understand. There is a hold it seems to have over us, this seemingly inanimate object, a command to follow the rules, obey the system. Queue just as good British folk should.

We watch as these two men fight it out in the middle of the road, grappling like toddlers, awkward and clumsy. It's a welcome distraction. They shove back and forth, until it becomes a standing wrestle, a fumbling tango. They're both a little podgy, red faced and wheezy, too long sitting down in cars and offices, so it's unsatisfying, humiliating even, but we watch all the same.

Eventually, the first man takes advantage of the increasing exhaustion of the second and manages to pull him into a headlock. He holds him there, triumphant for a moment, beaming idiotically, but quickly he seems at a loss with what to do with him, now he has won whatever it was they were competing for. He looks up at the sea of faces staring at him from behind glass, then releases him. They glare at each other one last time, then return to their cars.

There had been no indication this morning that the day would come to this. I woke at six, flicked on the television for the comfort of voices and nothing else, washed my hair in a shower puttering between scolding and ice cold and chose from the array of white shirts and grey trousers in my wardrobe. An urge to wear red quickly suppressed. I ate the same breakfast I've eaten for twenty odd years, drank from the same coffee cup, the rings of black inside a permanent marker of all the mornings I've had just like this one. I noticed the stain that's still on the skirting board in the hallway, despite repeated threats to scrub it clean, to paint over it. And before turning the key in the ignition, I returned to the house to check I hadn't left the gas on. Just as I have done every day for as many days as I can remember. I have never left the gas on, but once you begin a habit, it's hard to break it without feeling unstable. Without the floor beneath you crumbling. The routines are what keep us safe, what keep us from straying into the unexpected. So, you see, nothing out of the ordinary had occurred to prepare me for this. I think of my colleagues, sitting round the table, notebooks open, twiddling biros. I could ring. I should, perhaps, ring. But I won't.

There is a sudden screeching of tyres behind me and when I look in the mirror, I see one of the drivers from way back has decided they've had enough. She has pulled out into the other side of the road and is now driving at speed, alongside the waiting queue. She stares straight ahead as if her conviction could crumble at any moment, as if her resolve were wafer thin. She heads straight for the traffic lights, determination forcing the bone of her knuckles to reveal itself beneath pale skin. But just before she crosses over the lights and into the rest of her day, she suddenly and violently slams her foot onto the brake, the car lurching forward then back like a full stop, the mechanical scream shattering the silence. She looks up at the light, confused by her own abandonment. Pulls on the handbrake. Turns off the engine.

And that's the last of it. The last time anyone tries to defy amber. Something new begins to spring up from the cracked tarmac. A resignation. As if no one has the inclination to work it out. As if we are all tired of this treadmill.

I look across at the woman in the newly stopped car. She doesn't seem angry or irritated, just lost. Almost like she's forgotten where she was going and to what end. Looking at her it occurs to me that I have long hoped for something like this to happen. For an interruption to my every day. It's a relief, I realise. I feel as if I've been sleepwalking these past years, living a life on autopilot. There have been weddings and barbecues, holidays and Sundays. Moments away from the slog. But I've even dragged my way through those, as if they're just something to get through in order to get somewhere indefinable. A destination on the edges of a map I no longer own. I think, on reflection, I've been waiting for a crisis. Some terrible fate to befall me, something unignorable to pull me from this lethargy. I'm ashamed to admit it, but in the dead of night I lie awake hoping the morning might bring anything but the daylight; terrifying diagnoses, volcanic eruptions, apocalyptic disasters. Anything severe enough to change the course of my life. Being stuck at amber is not what I imagined. In comparison, a broken traffic light is a meagre, unexpected happening. If it can be described as a happening at all. Thin and sinewy when held against my imagined crises.

I realise now, sitting here in this traffic jam to nowhere, that this just won't do. This longing for a catastrophe whilst doing absolutely nothing to change. This isn't enough. This tiny life. Because what has it all been for? I have allowed the years to pass me by, swallowed whole by inertia. Waiting for something, anything to happen. Just as I'm having this thought, the woman in the neighbouring car looks directly at me. Not a casual glance in passing, or in the way strangers might search each other out in a situation like this, with a shared confusion. But in a deliberate way, an indication that she too feels this terrible dissatisfaction, this urgent need to blow up everything she knows. I am certainly late for the meeting now. There is no coming back from this. The pastries ordered ahead would soon start to dry up and curl. Like fingernails grown too long.

The person behind me turns off their engine, and one by one the other cars follow suit. A gentle clicking off, calming down, easing in. An acceptance of where we find ourselves. It's peaceful for a moment. There is clarity in this collective decision. When the engines have been silenced and we are left with only the memory of sound, a child on foot appears at the traffic lights. She is tiny. Maybe five or six years old. Inexplicably small for someone out on their own, crossing a busy road. She presses the button, looking up obediently at the amber, waiting for it to blush into red so that she might cross. We are all on tenterhooks. What might this small child do, this uncooked adult, this uncorrupted mind? She waits. We all wait.

Something catches her attention, a rush of sound or a lick of wind, and she looks to the sky. Her eyebrows knit together, she scrunches up her nose and then, as if from nowhere she erupts into a peel of laughter. The only sound in the whole world. Like bubbles bursting, like popcorn, like gunfire.

At this sight, people begin to leave their cars to see what has brought about this incredible reaction. I am suddenly aware of the soupy heat of my own car, and I too find myself opening the door, pushing myself up and spilling onto the road. I look at the queue behind and ahead of me, the same in all directions, a cross which seems to go on for miles now, further than I can see. The whole world stuck at amber. And beside each car stands a person, a person like me. We all look up simultaneously, at whatever it is that has delighted the child so much. And there it is. A murmuration of birds folding themselves across the sky like a sheet caught in the wind. An unusual sight for this time of the morning. They are purposeful, intent. As if they have something to say. One mind in a hundred bodies. They peel off the sky like a giant sticky label, then form the twisting loop of a helter-skelter. They flatten out impossibly wide, a fluttering flag, then narrow down to a pencil tip. A look of understanding now spreads across the faces of my fellow passengers. We have to do something. Because we haven't only been stuck at amber for the past half an hour, we've been stuck at amber our entire lives. Waiting. And for what? Waiting for it to turn green so we can continue driving toward the inevitable? Waiting for it to turn red so that we may lie down and die? There's a gust of wind, as if a giant has arrived at the top of the street and let out a sigh of relief. I feel it ripple through my hair, blow through my cheap suit. I look down at my feet, encased in leather, stifled. I bend down, undo my laces, pull off my socks and place my bare feet onto the tarmac of the road. When I look up, I see the traffic light has turned green, but no one shifts, no one retreats to the discomfort of their journeys. We all stand. We all watch the birds.

///inflow.evade.questions
by Conor McAnally

Sonny Bell had no friends inside. Allies, yes. Inmates who would side with him in a fight out of fear because here was a man who could end them in more ways than they could conceive. At least that's what they believed. Sonny walked the yard alone, boot kicking the odd, misplaced stone, surrounded by his vaporous breath, the mistiness of death.

He walked his walk and ate his meals, did his work, watched others steal cigarettes and contraband. He had no need of prison gin, no drugs or burner phone to ring. Who would he call? In all the world, there would be no one to answer. Sonny was a cancer, corroding every friendship made, his sex and companionship always pre-paid. He lived like DeNiro's character in *Heat*. 'Have nothing in your life so sweet you can't leave it in thirty seconds.' Smart thinking, Sonny reckoned.

He was a careful man, always had a foolproof plan for every contract he agreed. Every hit was guaranteed. He studied every mark's routine, searching for the magic time when he could strike unseen. Meticulous preparation. He always pulled the gun apart and threw the pieces in the river. But then he found a weapon he simply couldn't toss. He'd broken his own golden rule, forgot a gun was just a tool to be disposed of. He'd loved the look and heft and feel of the Sig Sauer. The power. But it was the gun that caught him. The ballistics tests revealed a bullet match and that key evidence ensured his prison stretch.

The days inside blended into weeks and months, everything the same, and no one messed with him until this one day when three big, tattooed dudes joined him at his table. He told them all to take a hike. It was his place, and they knew it. There'd be grief if they didn't do it. Their eyes told him right away he was about to get a kicking, but he didn't wait to figure out their reason. When the first one made a move, he smashed his tray into their faces, followed up with elbows, fast and without mercy. Wailed on them until the guards smacked him down to end the fight. The dudes just walked away. Something wasn't right.

He was dragged before the Warden, ribs aching from their batons, forced into a chair and held there. The Warden told his goons to go. Sonny was surprised.

'Mr. Bell will be no trouble. Isn't that so?'

Sonny nodded his assent. The guards and their batons left.

'A cup of coffee, Mr. Bell? Or tea? I'm a coffee man myself.' The smile fake, eyes piercing and intense. 'This is the first time you've been in trouble here, Mr. Bell.' The politeness was all pretense.

'Trouble didn't start with me. I just ended it.'

'I'm afraid you are mistaken. Trouble starts and ends with me. Think of it as a demonstration. I study killers, Mr. Bell, and you intrigue me. When I get to know you better, I may have a proposition for you to consider. But first, tell me about yourself.'

Sonny had been conceived in violence and endured his first beating before he escaped the womb. He'd grown up in two Texas rooms with a mother who'd forget to feed or clothe or bathe, more concerned about the needle in her arm than the squalling babe. A neighbor came once and pounded down the door, demanding answers. What was the baby screaming for? Momma Bell fixed her good, pulled out her husband's .45, pointed at the woman's head, told the bitch to go to hell or next time she'd be dead.

The boy soon learned to beg and steal, find a sucker, make a deal. Prey upon the weaker kids whose parents were a gentler kind than Sonny's whacked-out mom or his dad inside the State Pen for armed robbery again.

One night while his mother slept, he took the .45 and robbed a liquor store. Did it more out of challenge than of need. Indeed, he only got seventy-two dollars, but the adrenaline seed was sown and he robbed again, determined to get the cash for a gun of his own.

But these were not the things he said to the Warden, who was irritated by the bland tale of a deprived childhood which had forced him into crime.

'You're not being cooperative, Mr. Bell. You're wasting my time. Sad stories of your childhood are boring dross and filler. I want to know your path to becoming a dispassionate contract killer.'

One night in a grocery store the owner had fought back, pulled a .32 from underneath the till, shot him in the shoulder. Sonny blasted until the guy slid out of sight behind the counter. Sonny walked over, wasn't leaving empty-handed. He looked down into the man's glazed eyes and didn't feel a thing. And in that moment realized he might have a valuable skill. There was money to be made if he could kill at will.

His first mark was a distributor putting coke on Carmine Espinosa's patch. He had to be taught a lesson for the crew to watch. You mess with Carmine and you get two in the head. Dead. Sonny strolled up to the mark, put a bullet in each brown eye and walked on by, smiling at the payday he knew was on the way.

The contracts were infrequent but paid very well. Over time, Sonny expanded his clientele. Out of the streets and into the boardroom. Off the corners and into the bedroom. Cheating husbands and cheating wives, business partners brushed aside by a double tap with a .22. Problem solved. Just like that.

The Warden fidgeted as Sonny spun a yarn of hypothetical threads full of 'ifs' and 'maybes', aware that an admission might prolong his life in prison.

'Hypothetically,' the Warden said, 'if such a contract killer were at large, what would be the charge?'

'Twenty is a figure I've heard mentioned.'

The Warden leaned forward and whispered his intentions. Sonny listened carefully, smelled treachery and deception.

'I'm not sure what's really going on,' he said, 'but I for sure ain't playing.'

'There will be consequences, Mr. Bell.'

'I hear what you're saying.'

And so the pain began.

'Bell, pick up that cigarette,' the guard's breath hot upon his collar.

'It ain't mine. I don't smoke.'

'That doesn't matter.'

Whack, a baton on the legs, whistles blown and off to solitary. Back a few days later, a little bit more wary as the guards taunted constantly. 'Not much of a killer now — more like a loser.' There was no respite from the constant provocation, and the bruising repetition made Sonny turn darkly stubborn until —

'Bell, you got a visitor.'

'Who? I ain't expecting —'

'Law enforcement don't need an invitation.'

They marched him to the visitor room. Refusal was not an option. Beyond the glass was that bastard Sam Washington, the State Attorney man who'd put him in this prison, beaming like he was seeing a lover. Sonny sat down in front of the fucker, picked up the phone.

'Hey there, Mr. State investigator, did you miss me?'

'And a big hey to you too, Sonny boy. Bet you're glad to see me. How's life inside? I'm hoping it's miserable.'

'I get by.'

'That'll change soon. It's why I'm here. My office, we don't let things go, you know, we investigate for years.' He paused and Sonny waited, not reacting, wouldn't give this asshole the satisfaction. 'We found a witness, Sonny, and video confirmation. Remember the killing at the airport, in the parking lot extension? What we have now is no longer circumstantial. It might take us a month or two, but pretty soon you'll be strapped down for a lethal injection. I thought you'd appreciate hearing this information. Especially from me.'

Sonny looked him in the eyes and gave a little shrug, hung up the phone, and turned away before his face could betray him. He walked, banged the door and waited. Later, in his cell, he tried to catch the thoughts that swirled around his head. All the mocking voices saying he'd soon be dead. His father and his mother, the neighbors and their friends, all wandered round his dreams and said, 'You always were a useless man, a total waste of space, a blight upon the planet, a complete disgrace.' Sonny would wake up sweating, shocked at seeing his mother's needle arm and his own strapped down beside it—ready for the deadly mix that would kick him down into the abyss. Crazy notions surfaced, things he'd never done. He'd never been to Vegas, never been with a woman he hadn't paid for. As the days passed and the nightmares raged, he was plagued by the thought that he had never known love. Everyone talked about it, even those inside. He wanted to experience it, even once before he died.

Next time the Warden did his rounds, Sonny attacked, almost reached him before he was beaten back. Smashed to the ground, down, but angry now. He yelled as he was dragged away.

'One day I'll kill you, you and your whole family, and burn your fucking house down.' The Warden smiled at the brutal scene, happy that finally, finally, Sonny was playing.

What happened next was inevitable, mandated even. Sonny would be transferred to the Supermax in Livingston. When the day arrived, the Warden had to gloat. He had Sonny shuffled to his office, shook his hand, then grabbed his throat. 'So you'll burn my house down and everybody in it, will you?'

'Damn right,' Sonny croaked, 'first chance I get.'

They chained him in the prison van, the guard and driver both, not taking any chances. Twenty minutes later, Sonny collapsed and slumped over, held his breath till he was blue. The guard panicked, flew to the cage and opened it. Sonny jumped him, hands freed by the hidden key the Warden had firmly pressed into his palm. He clamped one arm round the shocked guard's neck, took his gun and shot him in the leg. The driver refused to stop the van, as Sonny knew he would. He dragged the guard to the window and shot him where blood and flesh would splatter, said he'd continue to shoot bits off and that'd be on the driver. The van stopped, the rear door opened. The driver stood there helpless. Sonny took his clothes and gun, radio and pride, shoved him inside and made him sit beside the first aid kit. He nodded at the moaning guard, said, 'Fix him, he don't need to bleed no more,' then slammed and locked the door. He put on the uniform and got in the driver's seat.

Sonny parked up near the Warden's house, climbed down, and scouted the location. Preparation was important, even though time was short. Three tan, unmarked cars had eyes on the old stucco mansion. They'd be armed and ready to kill without hesitation. Sonny changed direction, walked down a side street and pulled the driver's pistol, fired on two houses and into three parked cars, triggering alarms. The unmarked cars quickly relocated, searching for the escapee, but he was casually walking to the Warden's door. He rang the bell. When wifey answered, he caught a jasmine smell, blond, nice blue dress. He shot her in the face. Shame, he thought, she must have been pretty once. Then he stepped back so the doorbell camera would have a perfect view, raised both his middle fingers and mouthed, 'Fuck you.'

He dressed himself in the Warden's best and walked down to the kitchen, opened up the freezer and found the $20,000 where the Warden said he'd put it. Sonny turned on the gas burners and lit a small candle, picked car keys off a hook, took one last look and walked into the garage. He fired up the Warden's pride and joy, a '67 Gran Turismo. He drove away before the house exploded, showering debris all over the pristine neighborhood.

Sonny was cruising in San Antonio before the cops knew the car was missing. He had a solid exit plan if any hit went wrong. He drove to a lockup, dialed the combination, and hauled up the rolling door. Inside was a Ford Bronco and cartons stacked from ceiling to floor. Supplies for his cover business. *Bell Cleaning Corporation – We Take Out the Trash*. He pulled out three boxes of disinfectant to reveal his safe, full of cash, passports, and other papers. Sitting on the top shelf was a notebook bound in crimson leather.

He added a name to a long list and wrote on the next blank page.

I'm not the guy you need. I just do what people pay for. The folks that should go down are the ones who order up the killing. This book is a list of them, the businessmen and politicians, some law enforcement and the Warden. They're the guilty ones. I'm just the trigger. I'm done and gone. Not your problem anymore. Adios.

He wrapped the notebook in brown paper and smothered it with stamps.

Sonny switched the Bronco and Turismo, dialed the airport from a burner phone, and booked a flight to Vegas. He paid with a credit card in the name of Marcus Bell, a cousin who fell victim to an overdose. Sonny kept his identity alive, knowing one day it might help him to survive. He threw his go-bag in the Bronco and headed for the border. He ordered up two other flights while he was on the road, one for Miami and another for Philly. Disinformation, distraction, division of resources. They'd work it out in time, but time was what he needed. He stopped at a post office, put the package in a drop box addressed to the State Capitol for Investigator Washington. Job done.

Four hours later, he reached his destination, parked the Bronco on a side street and walked towards the river. He was dressed like a hiker with a backpack riding high. Inside was all he needed for his new beginning. Money and identity. Anonymity.

Sonny cleared the US side and started to walk across the bridge when a telephone rang behind him. He ignored the sound, knew he needed to make some ground, and started jogging. A guard stepped down from his booth, carbine at his shoulder. He shouted at his officer. 'That guy is an escaped prisoner.'

'Call the other side,' the officer replied. But the guard sighted down the barrel and fired. The bullet severed Sonny's spine halfway to his hips and as he slipped, a second round caught him in the neck. Blood spurted from his carotid, pulsing on the ground. He lay face down, knew that he was dying. His heartbeat slowing made him think of that damn grocery guy, the one who shot him in the shoulder. The man had been so stupid. His life was worth way more than the $500 Sonny put into his pocket. He heard the guard argue with the officer.

'He was a killer, heading for the electric chair, or needle, or whatever. Probably did him a favor.'

Sonny wondered if the guard had killed before or if he'd felt a thing—a ripple of regret, or guilt, or anything. His thoughts drifted, disappointed he'd failed miserably just when he was on the brink.

The last blood sputtered out and his brain began to sink into the abyss, just like in his dreams. Sonny Bell lay on the bridge, his final breath quite feeble, and wondered if his mother would forgive the overdose he'd put into her needle.

///hovered.loved.cried
by Emile Cassen

She doesn't feel much until she opens the front door and is greeted with the familiar smell, the comforting blend of good strong coffee, cigar smoke, antique rugs, and a hint of drains. Something about Dutch plumbing seems to lend this slight whiff to the houses here. Perhaps it's to do with the canals.

On the flight, she'd been fine. Tom had been more emotional, his lolloping sixteen-year-old frame apparently regressing, man one moment, child the next. He loves his grandpa. She'd been too busy with the practicalities to indulge the dull ache – the nascent grief: two weeks' worth of work to cover, childcare for her younger boys, and arrangements for the service. There's never a convenient time to die.

She'd written to the children's headmaster informing him, mischievously really, of the planned events. Tom would need to be excused twice – once for the death and again for the funeral. She could have spared the details but she wanted to shock him, to shake his English reserve with a hit of brusque reality. Nothing personal. She was simply kicking against conformity in all its tedious guises.

Arriving in England at the age of thirteen, she'd never quite fitted in, never quite managed to shake off the last vestiges of her accent. Her carefree certainties of acceptance and belonging had ended abruptly, stuffed awkwardly in a white polyester shirt, striped tie, black skirt and long black socks. Yet she'd settled there and was no longer at home in Holland either. She seemed to be forever uncomfortably straddling two cultures. Neither one thing nor another.

Up the stone steps to the front door, then the polished stairs to the apartment, her old key in the door. Ghosts of her former self, chattering happily beside her.

Her little group of friends would usually come to her home for lunch – throw down their school bags and kick off their shoes here – then make themselves sandwiches in the kitchen. How untroubled she'd been. How unaware of the transience of life as she knew it. A job in London. Her mother's career had been on hold long enough, she said. There'd been some arguing but the decision was already made. Her father was staying here, and they could visit him in the holidays.

Here he is. And her brothers and sister. Three kisses each, just like any other family gathering. In comes Evelyn. Years of practice have contorted her mouth, her predisposition etched into her features. In the lead up to today, they've all joked about the possibility of the needle accidentally slipping and taking her instead. Tacitly, they've wondered if they'd even need to be here now if it weren't for her. Why had he taken up with her? Maybe she suited his mood when they'd all abandoned him. Whatever his thinking, the choice had only isolated him further. Nobody liked visiting when she was there.

'Coffee?' Evelyn frowns and disappears into the kitchen, a short reprieve before her presence yet again blights their remaining time together. They're in an old argument. Her grievance – although it could have been anything – is that he isn't thinking of her, all on her own. He's being selfish. Her plaintive tones would sully any mood. His response: weary.

'Not this again. Sounds like you'll be better off without me.'

There's a break in their bickering when the GP arrives. He gently talks them through the procedure again. It's just a formality. They've been through it all before. It all sounds very civilised, but really, what are the chances of everyone affected agreeing that this moment in time – precisely now – is the right moment to die? Amongst the children, two are for, two against.

She's for – based on the simple premise that everyone should be able to decide for him or herself. No, that's too rational. She'll miss him desperately. A wave of desolation overwhelms her even at the thought of it. But if she's honest, this frail form in front of her has little to do with the father she still longs for: his hand on her back when he notices she's starting to flag on their long bike rides together; the stories of harsh wartime winters while he teaches her to skate, sipping thick pea soup from one of the makeshift stalls that pop up whenever these waterways freeze over; his reassuring presence at the side-lines, hands in pockets, at her hockey matches. He'd always been so energetic and now he can barely get out of the apartment. He can't even read. They've tried all the obvious solutions, but he doesn't want to be a problem that needs solving. He's had enough. A tiny unexamined part of her imagines this death will release the beloved father trapped inside this ageing misanthrope – the princess kisses the frog, the doctor administers his drugs...

As they start their goodbyes, Evelyn continues, relentless.

'Think of me! A widow! I'm not having it. What about my consent? He's not in his right mind.'

She grabs the doctor's case and leaves. The doctor runs after her – he has to, given its deadly contents. There's a short struggle in the hallway before he returns, flustered.

There's some small talk, some stilted laughter, until her father says, 'well she knows I'm not waiting for her. It's time.'

He embraces them all and says a few words to each. Then to the GP: 'We're ready.'

There's a bed downstairs now, where her mother's study used to be. He picks up a remote, lies down, and presses play. Mozart piano sonatas. Eyes shut, a tear pops up and rests there.

'Your mother used to play this beautifully.'

They know.

They're all holding onto some part of him – hands, arms, shoulders – as though they're caught in a storm and there's only one raft.

With the first injection, thiopental, he falls instantly into a deep coma. The second, cisatracurium, stops his heart. It's extraordinarily peaceful. She can't recall ever seeing him looking so relaxed. It's as though he's been released from something that had possessed him, and he seems blissful, almost beatific.

No one moves. They all stay on his bed – his four children, one grandchild, and the GP – until it's dark outside.

///games.smashes.throw
by Lily Devalle

It always starts here.
>On a Friday. Just after midnight.
>There's peace in it. There's torture in it.
>But you already knew this.

At times it feels like I'm stalking this place instead of the memory
of you.
>Running my hand along brick and mortar as if they were
>your skin, your hair.
>Inhaling sweet mildew as if it's the sweat of your neck.
>Maybe now they are one and the same.

Under the arch, I take shelter,
>Sit on concrete steps. Our steps.
>I take a moment, feel the slap of wind against my neck.
>Then I force my eyes up.
>Tonight, there's an eeriness to the tennis courts, the moon
>full above.
>But here, it is dark, the cave in which I dwell, from which
>I watch.
>A leaf swirls and scrapes across the green surface.

It taunts me briefly, circling your court.
My eyes follow its dance.
I swig from the perspiring Stella in my hand.

And here it is.
As if on cue, a vast space opens inside.
I can recognize it now, name it. An emotional riptide.
For a few lost seconds, it consumes me.
It blurs the edges of my vision. Distorts my hearing.
Suffocates my breathing.
Annihilates my rational thinking.

Two distant voices from the road behind drag me back to shore.
Their laughter, diametric to the agony in my head.
One says, 'Mate, you know her sister, with the fit little body.'
Fit little body. I smile, drop my head.
I said that about yours, didn't I?
An image unfolds before me.
That time it rained.
Me dry, watching. You soaked, playing.
The top, clinging to your body.
The white skirt, snapping with your swing.
The golden ponytail, heavy with rain, beating against your shoulders.

When I watched you some more, I noticed other things.
Those paradoxes of you.
The beads of sweat, glistening on sun-kissed skin.
Yet you were so *pure*.
The dickhead instructor, making you practice your backhand again and again.
Yet you were so *perfect*.

The laces of your trainers, coming undone.
Yet you were so *together*.

How I'd sit here, watching you.
Waiting.

At last, you came.
That day, everything changed.
I watched in disbelief as you followed the path around
the court, through this very arch.
You were drinking from your water bottle, but your eyes
were on me.
When you stopped next to me and sighed, I couldn't look
up.
Do you remember what you said?

A bottle rolls along concrete behind me.
It clink-clinks down nearby steps, and I know they aren't
far behind.
I pull my hoodie over my head.
Under its cloaking black, I force my body into stillness.
They take no notice of me as they claim the neighbouring
arch.

My fingers trail down the strings at my neck.
The ones you used to twist.
I pull one down, let it spring back.
And your coy smile appears in my mind.
My body starts to ease, my lips start to curl.

A glass explosion against the dividing wall jolts me.
My jaw clenches. My stomach tightens.
There's laughter, a stream of piss, echoing words.

They cut across my body like an X-ACTO knife.
I flip my hood back, crack my knuckles.
For a second, I contemplate rising. Walking over.

I fantasise about what I'd do to them.
God, would it feel good.
But mostly, what they'd do to me.
Shit, I'd even hand them the broken bottle.
Urban euthanasia, simple as that.

The voices get louder, but my heart fails to beat faster.
Adrenalin absent, fight or flight broken.
My body remains immobile.
But my eyes, my eyes stay active.
I survey the ground from wall to wall.
Yet my weapon of choice is already in hand.
I take another swig.

Yeah, you know well enough I can defend myself.
I don't remember much, those nights spilling from the
pub, you on my arm.
But I remember how you watched.
How you attended to me, wrapping bloody knuckles,
icing my face.
How I laughed off those displays, provoked partly to
impress, partly to release.
Now, the dead limbs by my side are the joke.

I sit some more.
Leaning on bent knees, inhaling ribbons of weed in the
air.
A dog barks in the distance.
A siren grows louder then trails off.

A car's headlights from behind sweep across.
A window slams in the apartment above.
And it strikes me as cruel, how such life can surround
such emptiness.
Life that goes on.

One bloke next door says, 'Life takes its proper beat, bruv.'
I repeat this quietly to myself, but it does my head in.
Like certain words that pound in my brain like an
aneurism.
The architecture here. The buildings in this complex. That
word you used.
Brutalist.
How it knots and twists now.
Morphs into something new.

I rub my palms into my eyes until they throb.
Then take a last swig.
I place the bottle next to me, against door 35.
Something causes it to vibrate.

How we used to joke about these storage sheds…
Why the hell outside? What the hell was inside?
'Probably electricals for the apartment block,' I said.
'I bet there are hidden bodies,' you said.

For a second, I hear stirring behind the door.
There's whispering. Or is it weeping?
But it must be in my head, in the wind.

My hands, knuckles chapped and red, are suddenly stiff.
I shake them back to life, then push my palms into my
thighs, kneading them like dough.

With a forceful exhale, I manage to half-stand.
I stagger to the bottom of the steps, lower to my knees.

Then I do something strange.
Like yoga or prayer on a mat, I fold forward.
I extend my arms, rest my forehead on the ground.
My fingers crawl along concrete with life of their own.
They search for the grate, its metal squares cold to the touch.
My fore and middle fingers curl and cling.
A cigarette butt rolls under my palm.
But I don't care.
Like succumbing to a bad craving, I have no choice in this.

The gravel pressed into my forehead is abrasive.
Turning my head, some pieces stick, others drop like sprinkles.
I press my cheek to the cool ground, ears pounding with your heartbeat.
Once again, we are lying here.
You in my hoodie, golden hair tucked inside.
Me pressed against your chest.

At last, it comes.
Tears cut trails along the grime on my cheeks.
I roll onto my forehead again, press my nose into concrete.
Inhaling you. Kissing you.
I don't fucking care if anyone sees.

My mouth opens and contorts, yet no sound follows.
My chest buckles, my stomach contracts.
Then an odd, low bellow is released.

An animal, injured.

Its pain bounces off brick, reverberates through.

Ricochets off apartment doors and windows above.

It startles even me.

The voices next door abruptly cease.

I know what I must do.

My body twists, an arm extends.

Fingers reach for the bottle, knocking it sideways.

Its echo is loud.

I grab the neck.

It jutters in protest as I drag it to me, smother it under my chest.

Footsteps and laughter draw near.

At last, they come.

There's a tingle in my chest as they surround me.

I don't look up, but can see trainers and boots from under my arm.

And there are three, not two.

My breathing accelerates, shallow and high in the chest.

One says, 'What the fuck you doin' down there, mate?'

Another spits, nearly hitting my face.

A moment of stillness.

Nothing moves, just my body with the breath.

I raise my hand slowly.

My middle finger even slower.

I wait for the first kick.

The first shattered rib.

I double over, the pain sharp and sweet.

Then I roll across the grate, face covered with forearms.

At last, adrenaline, endorphins, back from the dead!
I roll again, faster.
Firing out a shout, I spring to my feet.
I steady myself against a locker, orientate for a second.

I see them clearly now,
These strangers, all worthy opponents.
I smile.
They study me in return, eyes holding a glimmer of delight.
An early Christmas present.
I breathe out hard, and with a hand coax, invite them to dance.
Let's do this, assholes.
They close in.
Glass smashes against brick.

And here it is.
An emotional riptide.
It consumes me.
Blurs the edges of my vision. Distorts my hearing.
Suffocates my breathing.
Annihilates my rational thinking.

How fast it all goes.
How efficient it all is.
My head smacks against concrete steps. Our steps.
I hear shouting and pulsing and ringing. Then deafness.
I feel throbbing and fracturing and gashing. Then numbness.
I taste blood and salt and dirt. Then nothing.

But my vision, my vision remains crystal clear.

And it's you again.
That day again.

'You always look so sad. Like a lost puppy.'
  'Me?'
  'Yes, *you*. You know, the you who sits here, on this same
step, every lesson.
  The you who looks so sad.' You pause. 'Yet so *intense*.'
  I say nothing. I can't produce a sound.
  Not a single word.

How I've waited for this.
  Rehearsing it over and over in my mind.
  And now, I can't speak at all.
  I just swallow, glance up.
  Long enough to know you're smiling at me, those lips
slightly parted.
  And I want this moment to last forever.

'What are you waiting here for, anyway?'
  There's curiosity, amusement in your voice.
  I look down at my hands, knuckles chapped and red, and
smile.
  Then I look up.
  I meet those soft eyes.
  Eyes that soften me.
  'You. I've been waiting for you.' I pause. 'But you already
knew this.'

In this moment, everything contorts and shrinks
  And vanishes around us.
  There's just you and me.
  These steps.

This arch.
My vision starts to streak and blur around you.
Like a halo or the sky at dawn.

How it absorbs you — my vision, the streaks.
    My eyes lock tight with yours.
    Desperate, searching for forgiveness.
    I reach out, cup my hand around your neck.
    And gently, oh so gently,
    I bring your head into my chest.

It always starts here.
    There's peace in it. There's torture in it.
    And it was always meant to end here.
    But you already knew this.

///iterative.frantic.recital
by Ben Tufnell

Even now, so many years later, Iris cannot get the image from her mind. Once seen it could never be unseen. At night, it is always there: the hole in the ground like a mouth, and what lies inside.

The year she finished primary school her parents gave up their jobs and they left the city to go 'back to the land'. It had been a great adventure.

They lived on an old farm at the edge of a small village, and they kept goats and sheep and chickens and ducks. The house had been empty for years and there was a lot of work to be done. Their land was horribly overgrown. While her parents toiled to turn the crumbling outhouses and their few acres into a working smallholding, Iris was allowed to roam the surrounding countryside. Looking back now, she knows she enjoyed an extraordinary degree of freedom.

Only two places were forbidden. Next door was a big working farm separated from their property by only a low flint wall and a ragged hedge. Peering through, there were grain silos and cavernous barns roofed with corrugated iron. In the shadows within, she could see huge machines that bristled with claws and blades. It was made very clear to her that she must not go there.

The other place was the airfield. It lay about a mile down the road from the village. A wide-open expanse, once criss-crossed by grass runways, it was still ringed with coarse concrete tracks linking clusters of broken single-storey buildings and rusting Nissen huts, relics of the last war. Many years later Iris would learn to drive a car on those old tracks, but for now it was a forbidden place.

In that very long, hot summer, when all the green faded from the landscape, her cousins came to stay.

Two older boys, Danny and Lenny. She worshipped them. Her parents pitched a big tent at the bottom of the far field and that was to be their HQ. Danny, the eldest, had a tape player and cassettes of music. They carried piles of comics and books down there and lay around listlessly. The heat was too much.

Some days, they wandered through the ancient oak woods that pressed against the edge of the farm and the shadows there were the only cool places they could find. They climbed trees and built dens. The woods became their country, their land. Iris showed them the grisly fence by the track where the gamekeeper hung the corpses of stoats and weasels as a warning. The tiny bodies, in different states of decay, hung in the sunlight and swayed stiffly in a gentle wind. It was a breeze that brought no relief but seemed only to move the hot air around.

The fenceposts were topped with the bleached skulls of fox and badger. Lenny wanted to take one but she pleaded with him not to, saying it would be terribly bad luck.

They discussed the airfield. Let's go there, said Danny, who was mad for war stuff. We can't, Iris replied. It's not allowed.

But it sounds really interesting, Danny insisted. I want to see the runways and the tower. Maybe there are shells, bombs even.

Not now, said Lenny. They must have been cleared away years ago.

Iris was doubtful. But she wanted more than anything else to please Danny and Lenny and so the next day they set off down the lane and walked to the airfield. They had a rucksack with bottles of water and jam sandwiches wrapped in foil.

There was nothing to stop them entering, no gate or fence. They left the road and stumbled across coarse stubble towards a cluster of low buildings, the bristling remains of corn or wheat scratching their bare legs. They were soon surrounded by abandoned machinery but were disappointed to discover it was only old farm gear, a trailer, a plough of some kind, a pile of rusting barrels. Brambles and nettles. Mounds of rubble. Oil and dust.

The heat was incredible.

They peered in through one of the windows but couldn't see anything. Danny tried the handle of the door, but it was locked. He shrugged. I bet some of them are open, he said. They tried the other doors but they were locked too.

Wanting to impress the older boys, Iris bent down and dug with her fingers in the dirt, catching up some stones the size of eggs. Stepping back, she threw them at the windows. The noise of breaking glass was a shock.

The cousins joined in and a sort of competition arose. They took turns, shouting with jubilation whenever a pane was broken, groaning theatrically when they missed.

After a while they moved on and came to a row of Nissen huts which seemed to have been used recently. The brambles had been cleared away and there were no doors on them. The floors were pasted with dried mud and the smell of manure was overwhelming.

Barracks? suggested Lenny. Danny laughed. Smells like it.

Further on, they came to the only building that had more than a single storey, a square, blocky structure, very dilapidated, with large windows all around its top floor. They supposed it was the control tower, although 'tower' was the wrong word for it. It had been plastered and painted white, but most of the plaster had sloughed off, revealing breeze blocks and crude brickwork. The door was open and they went in, Danny leading. There were stairs but they were broken and unstable. Danny tried to go up but couldn't. Too dangerous, he said.

Two chairs sat facing each other in the empty ground floor space. Old newspapers lay around. Crumpled crisp packets. Cigarette butts. There was graffiti on the walls. Countless initials had been incised into the soft plaster and on one of the walls someone had painted a slogan – NO NUKES – and the CND logo. Someone else had scratched an A into it, to turn it into an anarchist symbol. They paused and drank water and discussed the proximity of the nuclear bases. The threat.

Jesus, this heat, said Lenny.

They crossed the concrete road that ran through the airfield and came to a squat pillbox. At that time there were still many of those strange structures dotted around the countryside. They bent down and climbed in through the narrow opening. It smelled of piss inside. When they came back out from the darkness the sunlight dazzled them and they had to shield their eyes with their hands.

Beyond, there was a dark opening, surrounded by thick brambles. A series of steps lead down and there was a grey metal door at the bottom. Danny tried the handle, but it was locked. I think this must be an air raid shelter, he said. Shame we can't get in there. Bet there's stuff in there.

At school, Johnny, who lived in the next village, had told Iris that there were tunnels beneath the airfield. She told the cousins.

We've got to find a way down there, said Lenny.

The heat and the dust. The air humming. In her mind's eye the sun is so bright and hot that everything is bleached. She squints and the memory of the airfield is a pale blur, fugitive oranges, yellows and, above, the pure blue of the sky.

They turned a corner and there was a wide area of concrete, punctuated by a row of raised structures, each at knee height and about four feet across, topped with rusting metal panels.

Danny inspected the structures. Tunnels, he pronounced confidently. If we can get this off we can get down there and explore. He was excited. He pulled at the metal lid but it wouldn't move. Crouching down he looked closer and could see that the rust had sealed it to the brickwork. He moved on to the next one and examined it. There was not much rust. He kicked and felt it move.

Come on, he said. I think we can get this one open.

The three of them began pulling and pushing at the lid. There were two handles, one on each side. It moved slightly.

Hang on, said Lenny. He ran over to the nearest building and poked about amongst the guts of some abandoned machinery, coming back with a metal bar. We can lever it, he said.

He worked the bar into the narrow gap between the lid and the brickwork. Then he began to put his weight on the bar, to lift the lid away, and the other two heaved. It shifted an inch or two.

Come on, said Danny. It's moving.

He counted them down – three, two, one – and they strained, and the metal lid slid across, revealing the dark hole beneath.

Danny wiped the sweat from his eyes, leaned over and looked in. Immediately he recoiled as if slapped, stumbling backwards.

Jesus, he said. Jesus.

What is it? asked Lenny. He too leaned over and looked into the darkness below and began swearing. He took a few steps away from the hole and sat down in the dust.

. Iris watched the two older boys and felt a ripple of fear pass through her. The sweat on the back of her neck was suddenly cold. Now she did not want to look into the hole but knew that she must. She wanted to walk away but knew that she could not. A long minute passed before she could move. Slowly, she leaned over and looked in.

Below was a vast chamber. At first the contrast with the fiery sunlight was such that she could not see anything, but then she could. Meat. It was a sea of meat. Flesh. Pink bodies, contorted, piled upon each other for as far as she could see, an ocean of bodies receding into the shadows. The sight was such that she felt her stomach turn over, as if something coiled up inside her had twisted in anger.

The heat. The air was like treacle. She swatted flies away.

She paused and was steady and looked down again. At first, she had thought it was people but now she saw that it was pigs. Hundreds of pigs. Tiny black eyes, mouths wide open. How deep were they lying upon each other? Iris could feel the coolness of the air rising from the chamber. And with it the smell: sweet, sickly.

Her stomach turned over again and suddenly she was on her knees vomiting into the dust.

Lenny's face was contorted in disgust. What are they doing in there? he asked angrily.

Maybe they're diseased or something, said Danny. He groaned. Maybe the farmer hid them in there. I saw something about it on the TV. There's a new disease.

The airfield was no longer a harmless place where they might muck about and have fun. It was no longer even an airfield. It had changed and they had changed with it. They all felt it.

Iris took the water bottle, washed her mouth out and spat into the dust.

There it was, right there. The other world. The new world where children could no longer be children. Where diseased pigs would be thrown into a hole in the ground and left to rot. She could not comprehend the chain of cause and effect that would lead to such an action. Even now, years later, decades later, it was awful to contemplate such matters. It was just too much.

Someone had put the pigs in there. Dropped their dead weight one by one into that black hole. The dead pigs were a nasty secret. They would do well to be away from that place as quickly as possible.

Somehow, they got the lid back on.

They never spoke of it again.

///poem.sorry.flown
by Billy Green

1st July '23

Sometimes love isn't enough. Sometimes the chase is the thrill, and the kill is an anti-climax. And it's been killed alright, our love has been killed. Sounds almost like a poem. I used to write poems about our love, in the early days. I still write some now in my notebook but keep them to myself.

Jon

'Jon? Jon? Can you hear me, Jon?' Someone was speaking to me, battling against the busker's song carried on the wind off the Thames. I opened one eye then the other, but closed them again when the blood stung, and I gagged when a coppery trace reached my mouth. I panicked then, tried to sit upright. The paramedic pushed me back down flat with a single hand. I was weak, I didn't resist.

I tilted my head. Light blurred in a hazy trail from the lampposts. I saw the feet of a crowd gathered around me, a loose circle, gradually dispersing as they realised I was alive.

'Easy mate, take it easy, you've picked up quite a cut there, we need to clean it out,' he said, firm but not unsympathetic, just not fully invested in what would no doubt be one of a dozen Friday night falls in London..

'Wha . . . what happened?' I slurred. I didn't know how long I'd been out, but my mouth was dry save for the drip of blood.

'You've taken a bang on the head. Can you remember anything?'

'No, no I...I can't. Where am I?'

'Control, we're bringing a male in, St Thomas A&E if poss, head injury...' he brought his clip-on radio closer to his mouth, the sound drifting further away...further away...as I slipped back into the black.

A white strip light. Silence. Then a beep. Then another. A pain in my neck as I tried to lift my head. Pressure on the index finger of my left hand. I lifted it to my face, a pulse monitor with a lead running to the beeping machine. The noise was a good sign I guessed. I rubbed my right hand against the crepe on my forehead, and winced. My lips were cracked. A nurse walked in then, wrote something on a clipboard at the foot of the bed.

'Good morning, nice to see you back in the land of the living,' she said, pushing errant hair back into a blue Alice band that matched her uniform.

'Morning. Can I have some water?'

She wrote something again on the notes, then picked up a plastic cup from the bedside table. I sipped it, spilt it, slid the back of my hand across my mouth.

'What happened, which hospital am I in?' I asked.

'OK, well that's good, you know you're in a hospital. How about you tell me your name?'

'Jon. My name is Jon.'

'Good. Well, we knew that from your notebook. No wallet I'm afraid but your Moleskine had your name and address on the first page. And a reward for finding it of fifty pounds – generous!'

'OK,' I faltered, 'so what happened?'

'Well, we don't know, but let me get someone to talk you through it. Bear with.' She spun on a heel and was off.

An hour later a deep voice resonated through the curtain. A policeman swished the green polyester to one side and gave a small wave of his hand, a gesture that seemed odd given his six-foot-five-inch frame.

'Hello.' One *Hello*, not three.

'I'm PC Willis. You've had a nasty knock on the head, can you remember what happened?'

'No. Again, no, I can't. Are you going to let me in on the secret, give me a clue?

I stopped then, calmed myself.

'I'm sorry, that was rude, I just can't remember, sorry.'

'Last night around eight pm,' a glance at his notebook, 'you knocked your head on one of the lampposts on the South Bank, the Mary Poppins ones along the edge. Probably saved you from going in the river.'

'OK. It's a blank.'

'A young lady phoned us.'

'Do you know who she was?'

He paused, flicked up several pages on his pad.

'We didn't get her name,' he said. I winced. 'But we took statements from some of the people hanging around. Apparently, she was stood over you, and had a *Rough Trade* tote bag over her shoulder. Oh, and dyed red hair. She shouted down at you – probably to see if you were conscious – looked around, snatched some blokes phone off him mid-conversation, made the call, then just…left.'

I was discharged that evening. I responded to questions about the current Prime Minister and my address, and as I didn't have any limbs hanging off, they let me leave. The NHS revolving-door system.

I took the Jubilee line from Waterloo to Canary Wharf, ignoring the private but loud conversations of boozers heading out for the evening, the questioning looks and theories of how I got the bandage on my head. It was still hot on the tube, the July heat lingering in the suffocating air. I was grateful for my discharge package of a bottle of water and two paracetamols, and I swallowed both in one hit.

I lived in an apartment in Sailmakers, a purpose-built tower block housing city professionals and privileged students. I turned my key in the lock and threw it into a gold bowl on the dark wood table inside the door. I was surprised at the muscle memory. There was another key on the floor; I put it back in the bowl with its twin. The flat seemed strange to me, but I sat down on an armchair by the balcony doors, sliding the cushion up the back of the seat a little, because it always snagged when I sat down. I closed my eyes and dozed. When I woke up the shadow from a tall reading light had eased up my leg. I'd been out for only an hour.

The grey kitchen had a kettle on the granite workbench. I opened the cupboard above it and flung a tea bag into a mug emblazoned with a *LamCap* logo. Again, I was startled by the ease of the action, but didn't recognise the company name. A MacBook sat on a low coffee table, and I logged on and opened Instagram.

Jon White, I was Jon White. My Insta tag read 'CityShagger'. I groaned and opened my posts. They were mostly pictures of me drinking shots with a bunch of lads. Ties undone, expensive suits. Crotch-grabbing pricks. In one photo – taken by a palm tree lined pool – I was standing behind a girl in a bikini, my face screwed up and my lips pursed, my hands held in front of me in claws. I closed my eyes, and wondered who I was. Wondered if I even liked myself.

In the bedroom I stripped, pulled back the mirrored sliding door on the wardrobe, and threw my stained clothes in the wash basket. Half of the rail was full of shirts and suits; the other half was empty.

The bathroom was clean, my aftershave lined up along the bottom of a mirror surrounded by lightbulbs. In the middle of the row was a pink bottle, it stood out against the rest. *Louis Vuitton*. Expensive. Clearly not mine. In the bathroom cabinet I found Alka Seltzer, Nurofen and a packet of condoms, one missing. There was also a key card from a hotel, stained white around its top edge.

Back in the kitchen, empty bottles wedged the lid of the recycling box open. Absolut, Tanqueray, Sipsmith. Vape tubes were lodged in between the gaps, cherry and watermelon. Who was I?

I rested on Sunday, called the office number on my business card on Monday morning. I explained that I had been in an accident and needed a fortnight off. A senior trader named Dick protested and sounded aptly named. I hung up, sat at my MacBook, and put an *out of office* on my email. I scrolled through the contacts list on my iPhone, searched for Mum or Dad, but came up blank. I couldn't bring myself to ring a contact I didn't recognise. Then I thought of the girl with the bag. I needed to find her. I was clearly not a nice bloke, but at least I could say thank you.

Rough Trade has three shops in London – East, West and Soho – and an online store. If she'd bought the bag online, then I was knackered. But I needed to do this good deed and thank her for hers, so that morning I took the Lizzie Line to hipster Shoreditch.

The shop was in an old brewery and sold books as well as records. And as the assistant told me, it's not *vinyl*, it's *records*.

'Boss, do you know how many red heads we get in here?' the assistant said, pulling on the end of his waxed moustache, before hitching up his 501s, even though they were held up with braces. It was Shoreditch, after all.

'Do you mind if I wait a bit in the coffee shop?' I asked, nodding towards the café at the side of the room.

'If you buy a cup, fella.'

Fella. This was going to be tough. From my social media posts, I wasn't a stand-up guy, but this rankled as much as *Boss*. I resolved to spend two days in each shop, East and West, and one day in Soho. And I would need my resolve if he called me *Bro*.

Whilst drinking my artisan Ethiopian brew, I used the time to trawl my Facebook photos. Annoyingly, there were gaps in the photo albums. I seemed to be pretty disciplined in posting most days – clearly the type of person who cared what people thought of me – but there were missing days, and no more posts after the holiday photos of a week in Bangkok with the lads last June. Had I really not done anything of note since then?

After lunch I hadn't seen a single red head, so I asked the fella what record I should take to the listening booth. My Spotify list had thrown up a playlist of club classics, curated by Ministry of Sound and Cream. I felt I needed something else in this place, something a little more cultured.

I slipped the headphones on and dropped the needle on *The Ballad of Darren*, Blur's latest release. The piano crept in, then guitars and I was swept away on melancholic vocals and triumphant strings. It was good, really good, so I bought it and made a note to buy a record player. By the end of the day, I'd worked my way through The Stone Roses, The Charlatans and The Smiths. It was magical, a guitar awakening.

But no red head, and I left feeling a weight heavier than the tote bag of albums I carried.

By Friday morning, having spent another day in East and two in West, I was feeling despondent. I'd taken off the bandage but hadn't shaken the feeling that I needed to shed the skin of the city trader with the swanky apartment and expensive habits. Listening to the music in the shops had felt like I was discovering myself, and I felt more strongly than ever that the red-headed girl was key to me moving on from the old me to the new.

So, I arrived in Rough Trade Soho late morning on that Friday, keen to finish the week off with a result, even if it was more albums. There was no coffee shop here, so I browsed a while then headed out of the door in search of a drink. Opposite was The Sun and 13 Cantons, an old school pub with a modern bar and restaurant at the back, with leather booths and a gold grid crossed bar at the back. Sitting at the table furthest from the door was a red-haired girl, and I knew it was her.

Mary

I saw him across the pub and stared until the heat from my Americano burned through my cup and into my fingers. I jumped slightly, instinctively putting my hands to my mouth, like a child pressing the radiator even though Mum said not to. He covered the space in quick steps, pulled himself up as he reached my table. I leaned back – he stood too close and, realizing, reversed a little, sweeping back his blonde fringe and revealing a fresh scar on his forehead, just above his left eyebrow.

'Sorry. Hi. Sorry, I'm Jon.'

'OK,' I said.

'What's your name? We've got the same bag,' he said, pointing to my tote.

'Yes. We have. You're very observant. Sorry, do you want something?'

'I do, I think you saved my life, the other night on the South Bank?'

'Oh, that was you! You OK? Well, of course you are, you're here. I'm Mary.'

'Do you mind if I sit down, buy you a drink, another coffee?'

'This one's still hot,' I said, 'but you get one and come sit down.'

Jon went to the bar and kept glancing over at me, as if he was worried I would leave. He came back with an Americano, sat opposite me, and put his bag on the table to his left.

'Let's see what you have then,' I said.

'What? What do you mean?'

'Your haul, what records have you bought, what music do you like?'

'Oh,' he said, his shoulders releasing. 'I'm really into Blur, love them, just buying the back catalogue. What you into?'

'Yeah, the same, I mean guitar bands, anything really.'

We talked for an hour, or rather Jon talked at me, garbled in a sweet way about how he was leaving his job – he worked in the City – and was going to use his savings to retrain. He didn't know what as, only that it would be 'worthwhile'. Jon asked for my number and he seemed different, so I gave it to him.

Back in my bedsit I thought about this stranger, this Jon. I lay back on my sofa bed – still out since my three-hour nap after my nightshift at the hospital– and thought about my last relationship, how it had gone so terribly wrong. I was on my own but not lonely, busy with work and saving hard for a move away, back home to Newcastle where I could rent a flat and not rely on my parent's pitying purse. I'd applied for a job at the

Royal Victoria Infirmary in the city, next to St James Park. I had two weeks to accept. Next door was cooking curry again, I wouldn't miss the smell.

My mobile rang. I jumped, startled, it hadn't rung for a while. *Jon* displayed on the screen, stark in the gloom of my small studio flat. I held the phone to my face, paused, pressed Accept – 'Hello?'

The next night we met in the Trinity Arms and sat in the garden, aglow with fairy lights. Jon had suggested going to see a band at the Electric Brixton. I hadn't heard of them, but they had guitars.

'Thanks so much for coming, I just wanted to do something to say thank you. I really do appreciate what you did for me that night,' he said, leaning earnestly into me, before pulling back and bringing out his Rough Trade bag.

'Here, I got you this,' he said, handing over the bag. I pulled out a copy of *Leisure*, Blur's first album.

'It's an original. They had one back at Soho, I went this morning to get it for you. It didn't cost much but . . .'

I put my hand gently on top of his, squeezed lightly.

'Thanks. It's lovely, a lovely thought. And it doesn't matter how much it cost.'

The gig was really good. We had a drink afterwards and he walked me back to the Tube. I gave him a kiss on the cheek. We're meeting again next weekend. I'll think we'll be alright, Jon and me. He seems nice. Nicer.

One week earlier...

'For fucks sake, Jon. You just don't see it do you?' Mary screamed. 'Swanning off all over the place, leaving me in your flat...your flat, where I have to clean up the shit you've left behind. You're a slob, a pissed-up prick.'

Jon swayed then, turned to Mary, anger rising along with the wash of the Thames onto the South Bank. He stepped into Mary's space, rocking forward on the heel of his foot. She pushed him back, just the flat palm of a hand on an outstretched arm. But it was firm enough to spin him around on his pivot, through one hundred and eighty degrees. And the pirouette was only stopped when his head hit the cross beam of an ornate lamp post. All went black.

Diary Entry Sep 23

I didn't mean to push him so hard. I just wanted to snap him out of it, bring him back around, not turn our lives around. I'd been flattered at first by his attention, impressed by the expensive gifts, the clothes and the perfume, the holidays. I had made the decision to leave him. Love had flown, never coming home. I'd taken all my things from his flat, posted the key through the letterbox. I untagged myself from every post, wiped our year long relationship from the internet ether. He knew I was going to County Hall that night, after my shift, to see Witness for the Prosecution. I was named after Agatha Christie's famous creation, the timid and shy Marple. That night I was neither, I was trying to get through to him, I just wanted to bellow through his distraction. But in the end, I broke, snapped in half.

I needed him to wake up and realise what he'd done. I could never leave him but I couldn't be with him with his behaviour and lapses hanging over us, not knowing when I would walk in on a party I wasn't invited to. I needed a reset, needed to give him a nudge, but I never thought it would turn out like this. I did it out of love.

But all's well and all that, he's here now, awake and back with me. He's trying harder than ever, harder than he ever did before. He actually loves me now. We've been seeing each other for three months, in our new relationship, our proper one. Sometimes love just needs a nudge.

> Most of the time we can pull off the bluff,
> Live our lives without thought, off the cuff,
> But sometimes it gets too much, gets too tough,
> And during those times, we need to remember;
> Sometimes love is enough.

///timing.part.waters
by Niamh McAnally

My twin brother, Rory, just went to jail.

'I suppose it was on the cards,' Dad said, wrapping his arm around my daughter, Sinead. She cuddled in and lay her head on his chest. It had been a while since my husband, David, and I had brought her over to see her grandparents. But nothing could have stopped us all being together in the family home this evening. Like old times.

I knew Rory going to jail was bound to happen sooner or later. Forty years ago, I wouldn't have cared. Back then, he got on my nerves – especially on Saturdays.

Mam would give us jobs to do around the house. I hated hoovering, and Rory knew it. He always *bagsied* doing the bathroom. After a quick wipe of the tub and toilet, Rory would be out on the road kicking a football with his mates. I'd still be hoovering in the sitting room. If Rory thought I could see him, he'd stick his thumb on his nose and waggle his fingers at me. He'd forget that Mam could also see him from where she sat at her sewing machine.

'Rory Kelly!' Mam would yell out the window. (My mother named him well, for she was always roaring at him.) 'Leave Deirdre alone.'

'Sure boys will be boys,' Dad would say. As an Aer Lingus pilot, he was rarely home on the weekends, but when he was, he liked a bit of peace and quiet.

One Saturday, after breakfast, Rory announced he would do the hoovering.

'There's a good lad,' Dad said, picking up his newspaper.

Mam muttered something, but stood up to wash the dishes. I skedaddled to get started.

When I finished the bathroom, Rory was still on the landing. For once, I'd get out to play before him. I gathered the coloured chalks I'd bought with my pocket money and closed my bedroom door.

'Have fun out there,' he said with his best Holy Communion smile.

He was up to something. I skirted around him, went down the stairs and out the front gate. I called to Annie's house, three doors up. She filled her dad's empty shoe polish tin with pebbles while I drew hopscotch on the footpath, white chalk for the outline and pink for the numbers. In the semi-circle at the top, I wrote the word HOME in bright orange. We were just ready to play when it started raining. Not drizzling, bucketing. Annie ran home, and I grabbed my chalks and scurried in the front door, absolutely soaked. And there was Rory, toasty warm, hoovering the hall, smirking at me. The little git. He'd obviously checked Dad's paper for the weather forecast first.

As we got older, we grew to like each other more. When we were stuck indoors, we'd make our own fun, sliding down the bannisters or wrestling in the dining room. Mam never said a word until that time Rory shoved me into the dresser, into the *good china*. Three of the plates wobbled off their perches and shattered on the floor. We both gasped. Shards of white porcelain with pink petals and slivers of gold trim lay scattered like a thousand-piece jigsaw no one would ever make. We didn't have to wait 'til our father came home. That was the end of horseplay in our house.

'Besides,' Mam said to Rory after she calmed down, 'your sister is becoming a young lady. You must treat her with respect.'

We were twelve. It made us both giggle.

However, when we were fifteen and Peter O'Leary tried to sneak his skanky hand up my skirt, Rory tackled him to the ground and I smacked Peter in the gob. Just the once. But, from then on, we were known as the *Scrappin' Kellys*. We didn't care what they called us, or that they steered clear of us. We had each other. Twins. We could *sense* each other's thoughts and *feel* each other's emotions as if we were the same person. No matter what scrapes we got in, we always found our way out. Together.

Change came when I started going out with my first boyfriend. I would talk to Mam about love and marriage and babies. Rory turned to Dad for company.

They fished on the river Dodder, supported Manchester United, and thought Jack Charlton was the best thing that ever happened to Irish soccer. Down in the pub, they'd sort out world politics over several pints and a packet of cigarettes. Dad hoped Rory would train as a pilot so they could fly together some day. And one day Rory did fly. Right after he graduated with a catering degree from Cathal Brugha Street Culinary College, he flew off to America to make his millions. I think it was the first time I ever saw Dad tear up.

Rory did well for himself, ended up managing posh hotels in the USA. During those years, he made lots of money and spent lots of money. He would come home every second Christmas with extravagant presents in fancy wrapping paper, spouting a new vernacular that made Mam roll her eyes. He walked on the sidewalk instead of the footpath, ate zucchini instead of courgettes, and got into all sorts of trouble offering Dublin women a ride instead of a lift.

Last year, he agreed to come home for good. It took a while for Ireland to settle on him again, but he stuck it out – for Dad, for all of us.

My husband and I almost have enough money to buy a house on Ailesbury Road. It's a stretch. Mam suggested we mortgage the property on Rathgar Road so we can come up with the shortfall. I was surprised. Mam doesn't say much nowadays, but when she speaks, it's worth listening.

She didn't go with Dad to visit Rory in jail. Mam was stuck on Grafton Street, off in her own world. As a dressmaker, she loved to window shop the latest styles. She used to remind me of those musicians who could hear a tune once and play it note-perfect right after. Mam would study those designer outfits, and without needing a pattern, she could fashion a replica that the average woman could afford. Eight years ago, she sewed her ultimate creation, the stunning silk gown Sinead wore to her Debutante Dance. Now, Mam takes comfort in twirling the thimble on her gnarled finger, a reminder of her passion and the profession that slipped away.

Sinead is a dote, and so patient with her grandmother, soothing her with gentle reminders when Mam forgets. Mam refers to Sinead as her favourite granddaughter, which is a bit of a family joke since she is my only child and, so far, Rory is still searching for the woman who can stop his head from turning. He adores his niece, and Sinead idolises him. She loves his spontaneity, his sense of fun and mischief. He is sweet with her. When she stopped at his hotel, she stayed for free. Me, he tried to charge.

'Rory says you owe him money,' my dad says.

I want to say Rory knows he's in no position to collect, but today's not the day to bicker. Today is about Mam and Dad. It

makes Dad so happy to have the whole family together again
playing Monopoly.

'Yay. Double sixes!' Sinead claps in delight. She moves her
iron twelve spaces. Rory throws and whisks his car around the
corner, side-swiping my dog.

'Hey!'

'Sorry Sis.'

'You can't get out of jail on a three and a four,' I say, putting
the metal dog back on the board.

Rory laughs. 'I borrowed Dad's *Get-Out-Of-Jail-Free* card.'

'That's cheating!' I say.

'That's Rory for you!' Mam says. Everybody laughs.

Dad puts his hand on Mam's arm. 'Cup of tea, love?'

Sinead jumps up. 'I'll make it.'

I nudge David, and he gets up, too. Out they go, closing the
dining-room door behind them.

And then it's just the four of us, Mam, Dad, Rory and me, the
original Kelly clan.

None of us knows quite what to say. The clock on the
mantlepiece ticks loudly. The same clock that used to herald our
bedtime with eight chimes. Now it counts these precious
moments. Rory and I want to stop the next tock. We want to hold
on to this moment, to keep living it, to stop it from becoming a
memory like all the other times we sat around this table. Oh, the
rows, the fun, the laughs we used to have. Rory always won
Monopoly, but Mam was the queen of Scrabble. It doesn't seem
that long ago, but we can see the years etched on Dad's face. Not
just age, but worry. Mam's skin is almost translucent, as if that
place her mind wanders off to harbours the fountain of
perpetual youth. She is disappearing there more and more,
staying longer each time. We know one day she'll slip in and
won't come out. I can see she's in there now, so I ask Dad about
tomorrow.

'Did you tell her?'

'Twice,' he says. He shifts in his chair. 'Perhaps I shouldn't go.'

'No Dad,' Rory says, 'you *have* to try. Please!'

'She'll panic.'

'Don't worry, Dad,' I say, 'Sinead will stay with Mam. Rory and I will go with you to the hospital.'

'Yeah Dad,' says Rory, 'the *Scrappin' Kellys* will be right by your side.'

Dad smiles. 'You were always good kids.'

He takes off his glasses and puts them on the table, then rubs his eyes. 'If it goes wrong,' he says, 'or the surgeon can't get it all this time . . .'

'Dad.'

'I want you both to promise me—'

'Dad, don't,' Rory whispers.

We know, and Dad knows, this is it. It needs to work. Mam can't lose him and we can't lose them both. Dad puts his bifocals back on; his magnified eyes remind me of an astonished child. I can *feel* Rory's tears well up and I want to thump him on the arm so I can give him an excuse to let them fall.

The door opens a crack. I hear a click, and the room plunges into darkness. My husband and Sinead come in, singing:

'*Happy Birthday to you.*'

Sinead's face is bathed in the golden light from eighty candles. Rory and I join in.

'*Happy Birthday dear Daddy, Happy Birthday to you!*'

Sinead puts the cake down in front of her grandfather. 'Make a wish,' she says. Dad sucks in a breath, but starts coughing.

'Don't worry, Grandad, I'll help.'

'So will I,' says Rory, switching on the lights. 'Let's get this party started!'

The two of them blow out the candles. Rory divides the entire cake into six ginormous slices, puts the first plate in front of Mam and plants a noisy, sloppy kiss on her cheek. My mother laughs. Then she frowns.

'Where's my thimble?' she asks.

'It's still on Nassau Street, Granny. Here.'

Sinead picks the thimble up off the board and places it on Mam's finger so she can twirl it round and around.

'Pass the dice, Rory. It's still our turn.'

David throws. The numbers roll up – a three and a four. I walk our dog the seven spaces and land on Chance. I pick up the card.

'What does it say?' Rory asks.

I pause. *'It's your birthday, collect €20 from each player.'*

'Liar!' Rory says, grabbing it out of my hand.

I try to grab it back, but as always, he is faster than me. He looks at it and laughs. I laugh, too. The more he laughs, the more I do. Then we can't stop. The pair of us are laughing so hard Rory starts snorting and my belly hurts.

'What's so funny?' Mam asks.

Sinead swipes the card from Rory and reads aloud:

'Go directly to Jail. Do Not Pass Go. Do not —'

Sinead laughs, so do Mam and David. Even Dad manages to chuckle without choking. Our whole family latches on to this silly moment. A moment of absurd hilarity in which we can temporarily escape.

Our last Chance.

Because when our laughter dies, and the room falls quiet, we can still hear the clock ticking towards tomorrow.

///outsiders.snakes.spillage
by Catherine Johnstone

(Content warning: violence)

Persephone was filled with a sense of wonder, and she reached out with both hands to take hold of the pretty plaything. And the earth, full of roads leading every which way, opened up under her. Homeric hymn to Demeter.

Ask me if I remember that night nineteen years ago and I will say I remember the sweet play of Alex's fingers darting across my ribs. Ask me if I remember the softness of his inner elbows where he writhed at the tickle of my hands, and I will say yes. Ask me if I still taste the syrup of his breath as we kissed, and I will say yes.

At the hut in the beginning, my head was clear, and I knew what I was doing. I said yes to him that night. I remember that. He rocked me even though he grimaced in pain with the cuts on his stomach. His skin was warm by then and he asked me if it was okay, and I said yes. I remember the shock of him in my body even though I kept saying yes.

Ask me when the Fanta and vodka became sickly, and I will say I don't remember the exact moment, but sometimes when

I'm in a pub or a cafe, my nostrils still flare with it. Ask me if the bitterness of those pills swells thick on my tongue and I will say yes. Ask me if I still hear the thrash of branches and the wrench of the roof lifting off the hut in the darkness and I will tell you that when there's a storm at night, I wake with the sheets twisted, and sweat on my cheeks. Ask me if I remember a dank mine and sharp fingers and I will say that part is as dim as a shadow. Ask me if I remember the sodden struggle back home and I will say, I remember it when rain falls on my hands and seeps into the hair on my scalp.

***

That night I nudged open the screen door and eased it shut so it wouldn't bang against the frame. My full backpack jolted against my spine as I jogged past the squawking cockatoos in the branches of the peppermint gum. Before I sneaked out of the house, I'd shoved in a packet of biscuits, three apples, tuna, my sleeping bag, parka, torch, matches, Swiss army knife and a water bottle. Too much for one night away, but better to be safe. I flung a glance over my shoulder. Good. Neither Mum nor Dad was following. I'd teach Dad a lesson: it would serve him right when I didn't come home. He wouldn't even care. Mum cared, but she was the other extreme: over-the-top protective, though I was sixteen. She wouldn't even let me stay overnight at my friends' houses.

Ripples of purple and slate-grey clouds massed on the horizon. I hoped it wouldn't rain before I got to the hut on the hill we called the mountain. In the home paddock, the smell of manure leached out of the milking shed into the early evening. From the odour, I knew the cows had eaten the rich grass from the paddocks rather than hay. Inside the double doors, stainless steel cups and rubber hoses swung from the line. Ha! I wouldn't be there in the morning to shove cups onto the poor cows' udders for the millionth time. I'd show Dad. Tomorrow he'd have to do the milking on his own or ring Hired Hand Harry as I called him. Harry was always at Dad's beck and call. Just as well I wouldn't be there when he came.

I'd always fought with Dad, but our argument that night at dinner was sharper and louder than normal. He acted as though I was being unreasonable when I told him I didn't want to do as much on the farm, I wanted to study and didn't like him shouting at me all the time. When he got angry, flashes of rage ripped across his face like lightning. One minute he was chewing a chop and the next, he was yelling. Mum would say, 'Stop, Zane!' but nothing she said made any difference.

My riding boot plonked into a water-filled pothole edged with tractor ruts. Circles formed around my boot, and mud splattered onto my jeans. It was after seven but heat still pulsed from the land. It gathered in the odour of the perennial ryegrass, the sweat that darkened my check shirt and collected under my Akubra hat.

I darted a look towards the house, but no-one was following. I strode onwards. By the time I reached the ghost gum, sweat trickled down my face and my inner thighs were chafed from the rub of my jeans. A gash in the trunk oozed with blood-red sap.

In the far paddock, cows bellowed for their calves. I hated that they were separated soon after the calves were born. Dad said I should toughen up and be a proper country kid, but I couldn't. In the near paddock, the silage cylinders on the shorn grass looked poised to roll away. Once, Alex and I climbed up and lay across one. I tickled him and we rolled off. He inhaled the powder from the hay and coughed so much, we killed ourselves laughing. Warmth flushed through me and I wished Alex was with me now.

Beside a Scotch thistle, an iron vice was half-hidden in the grass like the jaws of a fossilised animal. My hands twitched to pick it up for my collections, but I couldn't carry it, even though it would be a good match for the iron hook I'd found rusted into the ground.

A spur-winged plover screeched, and I jumped. The weight of the backpack dug into my shoulders, and I heaved the straps up to ease the strain. Ahead of me, the eucalypts of the State Forest formed a wall at the boundary of our property, and the canopy extended up the incline. At the fence, I unhooked the loop from the post and swung open the gate. I plunged into the half-light of the forest and trudged along the old pipeline track. The eucalyptus trees exuded a pungent scent as they rustled in the breeze. I heard a swishing sound and peered into the gloom. Something or someone moved. My knuckles whitened as I gripped the straps of my backpack. Maybe it was a bad idea to run away from home for a night, especially when the clouds hung grey and heavy.

I inched up the track and saw the source of the sound. A split branch dangled from a lemon-scented gum like a broken arm. I startled as it clattered to the ground beside the track.

I had forgotten to wear my watch, but when I got to the dam, I could tell by the fading daylight it must be about eight-thirty. Dust had mingled with the sweat on my face and my legs felt sticky under my jeans. I wanted a dip in the cool water. Near the dam, someone had left a Fosters can and a deflated swim ring covered with faded octopuses. I flung off my backpack and clothes and left them in a heap on a log. My hat rolled onto the stones. Mud squished between my toes, releasing a marshy smell as I picked my way around the kangaroo poo and reeds on the bank. The pollen clouding the surface dissipated in the tea-coloured water. I sank down and the water sluiced away the dirt and sweat on my body.

As I stepped out of the dam, I shook my hair and arms, wishing I'd brought a towel. The purple-black clouds spread across the sky and the temperature dropped. Better hurry up and get to the hut before it turned pitch black. I wondered whether Mum had noticed that I was gone.

Still naked, I picked my hat up from the ground where it had blown away. Behind me was a thumping sound and I jerked around. I squeezed one arm across my breasts and covered my pubes with the other hand. My shoulders tightened as I peered into the forest.

'Is anyone there?' I yelled.

A wallaby ducked and weaved out of the bush as though escaping from something. Startled eyes darted towards me before it hopped away. I shimmied into my underwear and clothes, the shirt still clammy with sweat. I tried to wipe the mud off my feet before I put on my socks. I slung on my backpack and strode onto the dark track. The bush clattered with creaks and shuffles and whispers. The wind picked up and a soughing sound hummed in the canopy. Leaves scurried around the earth. The call of an eastern whipbird cracked around the bush and died away. Thumbs under my straps eased my aching shoulders. The track incline increased, and I slipped on loose scree. Raindrops pattered on my Akubra, and I stopped to get out my parka.

A lightning fork flashed in the darkness and lit up the Danger sign on the orange pipeline pole beside the track. Just my luck. A thunderstorm. It was dark but I didn't want to use up my torch batteries. I edged closer to the first pole and peered into the distance to find the next one. I quickened my pace, even though the track was steeper. I bent my head as rain stung my face.

I forged upwards past the cluster of blackened trunks from the 1983 fires, with leaf litter and dried twigs scattered around them. Not far now. At least work on the property kept my calf and quad muscles strong. By the time I got to the summit, it was black and the lights of the town on the other side of the mountain formed haphazard dots and lines. Lightning streaked down from the roiling clouds like yellow tentacles.

If someone had watched me from behind the trees, they would have seen determination in my shoulders, the rise and fall of my Akubra, fair hair flung down my back. But if they had seen me many hours later trailing down the mountain, arms draped around the shoulders of two boys, they would have seen a broken thing, a stumbling thing. They would have said, what happened to your strong legs, why are you mumbling and where did you lose your Akubra so that now your hair hangs limp and rat-tailed? What has happened to you, little one? What darkness has scratched your face and inhabited that head? Why do you groan and smell sickly-sweet? They would have heard the heavy steps of the two boys, the crack of twigs beneath their feet.

I arrived at the edge of the clearing and stared at the hut. Flickers of light flashed from inside it. Who could be there? The rain pelted and the wind buffeted me from all directions. My jeans were drenched, and rivulets of rain trickled off my backpack. I looked back at the oppressive blackness behind me. I couldn't go home now.

Come on. Don't be a wimp. I edged towards the hut. I hoped whoever was inside couldn't see me in the darkness. I peeked through the grimy window but couldn't see who was there. The pulse on my wrist drummed. I pushed open the door.

'What are *you* doing here?' Light from a small fire darted across Alex's smiling face as he sat on a wooden bench.

I laughed. 'Hi, Alex. Ran away. Another fight with Dad. What are *you* doing here?'

He grinned. 'A quiet night under the stars, would you believe?'

'I'd believe it, you astronomy nerd you. Should've checked the weather.'

I sat beside him. The flames lit up a cut on his forehead and blood smudged along his cheekbone.

I gasped. 'What the fuck happened to you?'

He shrugged and winced. 'A long story about a water bottle and the creek.'

I glanced at the floor. Drips from his soaked jeans formed a puddle. He jerked in a fit of shivering.

'Better get out of those wet clothes.'

He eased off his coat and wet hoodie. The flesh over his ribs was gashed.

I wrapped my sleeping bag around his shoulders and pointed to his jeans. 'All of it.' I pretended to put my fingers over my eyes, blinked at him and chuckled. 'Promise I won't look. Unless you need help?'

'I can do it.' He winced as he bent forward to unzip his jeans. I looked away.

Side by side we gazed at the fire. He pointed to a backpack at his feet. 'At least I didn't lose this.' He unzipped it and brought out Absolut Vodka and a bottle of Fanta. 'Want some?'

'Sure.'

We downed vodka and gulped codeine tablets that Alex had taken from his father's medicine cabinet. Our voices slurred and orange liquid stained our lips as we dribbled with laughter. We fed the flames. My fingers trickled across his chest. His hand slipped onto my thigh. While the rain teemed onto the roof, we giggled like we were twelve years old.

The rain was the beat of a drum and our bodies felt wild as if the wind swept through our blood. We blared out the words of SOS and I jumped up to dance. Alex wrapped the sleeping bag around his waist and danced too. Light and jagged shadows flashed around us as if the scene was a primitive ritual. The sleeping bag fell off Alex's waist and his penis flopped in the flickering flames. I was shy but ready. I flung my arms around him. He stumbled and I remembered his gashes and held him gently.

I threw the sleeping bag on the wooden bunk. My blood pulsed and sang, and the rain pounded, and I pulled him to me. I still had my clothes on, and he said, 'you're wet' and I dragged off my shirt and jeans, and his body was warm. We lay together while the trees tore at the air, something slammed on the ground outside and thunder banged across the land.

I imagined drifting above us and looking down. I saw the pull of Alex's toes against the blue of the sleeping bag, the flash of my breast, my ropey back muscles strong with the hold of him, the ripple of his biceps in the firelight. I saw my hair flung across his skin, a squashed Akubra on the ground, disembodied jeans, the glint of firelight on the Absolut bottle on the floor. I smelt wood smoke and orange soft drink, Alex's sweat, the earthiness of the hut. I heard the creak of the roof, the strain of nails against wood, the force of the wind nudging at the eaves, the jerk of the corrugated iron.

When the roof blew off, we were pounded with rain. The fire sputtered and we bumbled around in the dark. I was thick with vodka and pills. We dragged on wet clothes and grabbed our backpacks. Alex found his torch and yelled above the wind.

'We can go to the old mine. It's not far away.'

Ask me if I remember the stumbletrip of our journey and I will say I remember the red of the whipping wind that flipped back my hood and the rain lashed my scalp and filtered into my Docs. I will say I remember the haze of it, the daze of it, the wet of it. Alex lurched ahead of me through the bush. In the darkness, his torchlight veered through the trees like a mad animal. The undergrowth scratched at my hands and my head whirled and I wanted to lie down in the wind and rain, and sleep, but Alex kept saying, 'Come on, Pip, come on!' Ask me if I remember the mine entrance looming like the mouth of a giant wolf and I will say yes.

But ask me about that night after I fell in a ragged heap on the earth of the mine and I will say, I see it in shadows, I hear it in grunts and groans, I smell it in puffs of stale air.

Ask me if I remember Alex turning on my torch and leaving the mine to pee and I will say yes. Ask me if I remember how long before he came back and I will say no. Ask me if I remember someone else coming into the cave and I will say yes. Ask me if I remember what happened then and I will say I was made of rags and my head was thick. But I do remember I said, 'Stop,' as another boy's spiky hands pulled at my clothes. My back felt jagged as it hit the hard dirt again and again and I called out, 'Don't. It hurts.' Ask me if I remember whether it was Harry and I will say, 'Yes, I saw him when the torch rolled and lit up the sharp lines of his face.' Ask me if I remember when Alex returned to the cave, yelled at Harry to leave me alone, and I will say yes.

Ask me if I remember Harry and Alex supporting me back towards the hut and I will say I remember my feet dragged over twigs, snaking roots and stones. My eyes closed as we neared the hut and I said, 'Let me stay here, let me be,' and Alex said, 'The roof has gone, you can't stay here,' and Harry hoisted me onto his shoulder like an unwieldy sack and my stomach mashed against the ridge of his muscles. I remember I muttered, 'Harry, where did you come from?' and he replied, 'Your father rang.' Alex kept saying, 'Are you okay, Pip?' and I would open my eyes to see his hands flutter in the air. I should have felt wet clothes plastered against my skin, but I couldn't. My skin was empty.

And back at the farm when Harry told Dad he found me, and he dumped me on my bed, I was numb and barely-there. I whimpered for Mum, but she didn't come. She had driven towards town to find me. I don't remember what happened then except I slept for hours and hours as if I was dead. I was only sixteen and sometimes in the following year, I wished I *was* dead.

In that year, I birthed my boy, I gave him away and my mind went astray.

I didn't live again until I fought back. Harry was charged and I was glad.

These days I say to myself, make peace with the child you were. You were only sixteen, vital and soft-skinned, ready to live a full life. Make peace with that child who played in the warming hut, with that warm boy. He was a trembling boy, and you were a trembling girl and neither of you had drowned in another's spit and lick. You were both shiny children who wanted to explore bodies. At that moment, you didn't know the harm one body can do to another, the harm that another boy's body would do that night. Sure, you knew the harm that words could bring, even the words of your own father, but you didn't know that by the end of that night you would no longer be a child.

***

Today, my feet glitter with grains of sand in the morning light and the sea air hums around me. I look out across the lagoon and breathe in the wonder of this new place, far away from the now-desiccated country of my youth. I have another child now, but the child I lost hides inside my chest. I wish I knew him, could make him as real as the clothes I wear so I would not feel the nakedness of his absence.

When you look at me, you cannot tell I slipped into the mire that long ago night. But I see lines on my face that cram together like the topography of a wild mountain. I can't undo the thin shadow of my skin.

A grey-brown sandpiper swoops onto the sand.

Sometimes I don't know whether to be glad or sad that my son was born. Either way, I don't know him, the joints and flare of him, the pulse and warmth of him, the eighteen-year-old smell of him. Is he watching a bird this very moment or kicking at tufts of grass on the edge of a soccer field?

The sandpiper's head bobs as he pokes into the wet sand beside the lagoon. I can't see a worm or a little creature in his beak each time he comes up. It's as though the drops of food are so small, they barely exist, but that is enough to keep him strong, to keep him pecking at the sand on a golden sunrise morning.

A Note from Anna Davis
Founder and Director of
Curtis Brown Creative

When Niamh McAnally contacted me recently to tell me that she and her writing group had written a themed book of short stories together, and that this anthology was shortly to be published, I wasn't the least bit surprised. And this lack of surprise was irrespective of the fact that it's very difficult to get collections of short stories commercially published, no matter how good the writing – and that it's even more difficult to find a publisher for a book with multiple authors, most of whom are previously unpublished in book form.

My lack of surprise was precisely because it was *this* group of writers.

At Curtis Brown Creative, we run long and intensive courses online and in London where students are taught by acclaimed authors and given publishing advice by literary agents and other professionals – and a goodly number of these writers end up getting publishing deals. Lots of our student groups bond and become trusted readers for each other for the longer term – and I've come to believe the peer group is the absolute most useful thing we have to offer writers on our courses.

What's more unusual though, is that *this* group of writers first met on our Edit & Pitch Your Novel course – it's a much shorter online course, and consequently there's nowhere near as much opportunity for its students to make lasting relationships. And yet this group, drawn from across the globe and with very differently shaped lives and writing projects, has done just that! It takes real dedication and staying power for a group to bond like this across time zones and despite all the pressures of busy lives – and to then have got together for an actual physical writing retreat in the UK is a significant commitment which they somehow all signed up to.

So, yes – it is no surprise, really, that *this* group of writers should be publishing a book together – and that Niamh, who is absolutely a Force of Nature, is there at the helm.

May there be many more published books to follow, both collectively and individually, for these talented, determined, innovative and mutually supportive writers.

–Anna Davis

About the Authors

Emile Cassen

Emile Cassen (pen name) is a scientist, a mother of four, and lately a writer of literary fiction. Originally from the Netherlands, she studied Natural Sciences at Cambridge University and completed a PhD in cancer research in Berne, Switzerland, where she fell in love with the mountains and spent every spare moment ski touring and mountaineering.

Emile worked for many years in research and education, but during a protracted divorce, she found herself compulsively writing about the experiences she was struggling to process. Short cathartic stories about life as a mother, a scientist, a wife, and the factors that can lead to a spirited educated woman becoming intransigently stuck. These themes were eventually incorporated into her novel, *The Shadow of Pure Light*. Emile was signed by a top London agent and the manuscript made the final shortlist of the Dundee International Book Prize. Other literary credits include being shortlisted for the Ruth Rendell short story competition.

Emile lives in Kent and teaches healthcare professionals. When she's not working, she enjoys playing tennis, walking her dog, and still goes skiing whenever she can.

Instagram: emilecassen

Lily Devalle

Lily Devalle (pen name) is a clinical psychologist from New York, where she obtained her Ph.D. and work experience in diverse clinical settings. She now runs a private practice in London, UK. Her media portfolio includes the *BBC, The Guardian, The Huffington Post, Psychologies* and *The Telegraph*. She has published academic papers, magazine articles, blog posts and a self-help guide.

In recent years, Lily has turned to creative writing to present mental health issues in a more entertaining format and challenge stigma on a larger scale. Her debut novel, *Confessions of a Female Stalker*, yet to be released, is a dark psychological comedy about a young professor whose infatuation derails her seemingly perfect New York life (*The Girl on the Train* meets *Sex and the City*). She is developing a second novel, *The Strange Bright Days*, which explores the spectrum of mental health and identity issues in an entertaining romp through the glamorous (and sometimes not-so-glamorous) world of 2000s Manhattan. Lily's passions include travel, yoga, fitness and martial arts, particularly Taekwondo, where she holds a third dan black belt. She is also a supporter of UK organizations such as the National Theatre, the Almeida Theatre and the Women's Prize for Fiction, along with various animal rescue charities.

Instagram: @golden.notebook

Sandy Foster

Sandy Foster is an actress, novelist and playwright. Her plays have reached the final stages for several writing prizes, including the Verity Bargate Award, the Bruntwood Prize, the Women's Prize for Playwriting, Theatre 503 International Playwriting Award and the Royal Shakespeare Company's 37 Plays. Her debut novel, *The Weight of All of Us*, explores what it is to be facing the destruction of the species at our own hands and puts the very real threat of climate change centre stage. She is represented by Philippa Sitters Associates who are currently pitching to publishing houses.

She is passionate about putting women at the heart of her stories and is preoccupied with the big moral questions facing humanity. Having grown up in the coastal town of Bognor Regis, the sea is a constant feature in much of her work. As an actress, she has worked extensively both onstage and screen, most notably with the award-winning film director Mike Leigh, the Royal Shakespeare Company and in Disney's recent remake of *Snow White*.

Sandy enjoys long distance running and cold-water swimming. She is based in London with her partner Bill, and mini dachshund, Rita.

www.philippasitters.co.uk

Billy Green

Billy Green was born in Northumberland and joined the Royal Air Force at 17 (the only other option being working underground down the pit) and served for 13 years, including 8 months in Desert Storm.

On leaving the RAF, Billy moved into sales and travelled extensively around the globe for business, including a spell in 2004 to lead a team to Indonesia to recover communications after the Asian Tsunami, during which he hard-landed in a helicopter, spent the night with a tribe in the rain forest and rescued 90,000 people on Simelue Island.

In 2020, Billy released 'Still' as BillyGreen3, an album of songs charting love and loss in a relationship, writing the songs, singing and playing all instruments. A second album 'Gazelles' expanded on the theme and followed in Dec 2023, and was entered for the Mercury Music Prize.

All of these adventures and the albums have been used as the basis for BLINK, a contemporary thriller. Always keen to develop as a writer, Billy adapted BLINK to a screenplay and was one of fifteen selected to attend the six months Curtis Brown Drama Screenwriting course. This has expanded his writing tool kit and network of contacts.

Instagram: billygreen333

Catherine Johnstone

Catherine Johnstone is a queer writer living on Wurundjeri land, in Melbourne, Australia. Her writing has been published in Australian literary journals such as *Westerly*, *Meniscus* and *Going Down Swinging* and an anthology, *A Remarkable Absence of Passion*. She was awarded a 2022 online Varuna fellowship, *The Writer's Space*, and a 2023 KSP fellowship. She was short-listed for the 2024 City of Melb Narrative Non-Fiction Prize.

She writes fiction and creative non-fiction. Her memoir manuscript features hybrid pieces that investigate the mind, the body and non-violence, within the context of her own experiences. Her stories in this anthology are fiction and not based on actual events or people. *Outsiders/snakes/spillage* draws on the Greek myth of Persephone.

Catherine has had previous successful careers as an artist and short film writer/director. Her short films screened nationally and internationally and won awards such as Best Australian Short Film (Melbourne Queer Film and Video Festival). As an artist, she has had exhibitions and won art awards such as the Fiona Myer International Travel Grant to travel to Italy.

She has received grants and funding from Australia Council, Australian Film Commission, Fiona Myer and Myer Foundation, Melbourne Queer Film and Video Festival, National Association for the Visual Arts, University of Melbourne and Victoria University.

Photo credit for image of Catherine Johnstone: Bree Dunbar
www.catherinejohnstone.com
Instagram: cath.johnstone

Conor McAnally

Conor McAnally is an award-winning writer, performer, producer and TV director. Irish born, he is a former investigative print, radio and television journalist. He has produced thousands of factual and entertainment television shows for networks worldwide including BBC, ITV, Channel 4, DirecTV, AMC, Nickelodeon, RTE, SBS, Fuse. His TV shows have garnered twenty-two major awards including five British Academies (BAFTAs) and five from the Royal Television Society.

In TV drama, McAnally created, wrote, produced and directed the hybrid youth drama series *Over The Wall* for BBC. In theatre he wrote and performed three one-man shows – *The Irish in America*, *Texas Independence* and *The Mexican-American War*.

Conor's flashfiction work *Love Spines* won the Plaza Microfiction Prize, 2024. Short story *The Psychiatrist's Window* was a prize winner in the South West Writers short story competition. His first novel *Bullets In The Water* will be published by Stoney Creek Publishing in 2025. His next two projects are an international thriller involving Irish special forces, and a historical thriller during the California Gold Rush. Conor's passions include skydiving and gardening, motor racing and cooking, motorcycling and walking, golf and poetry. He and his wife Kay have homes in Austin, Texas and Galway, Ireland.

Website: https://www.conormac.com

Niamh McAnally

Niamh McAnally, known as The Writer On The Water, is an Irish-born award-winning author, keynote and guest speaker on Celebrity Cruises, and former TV director. As an avid explorer with a penchant for volunteerism, many of her stories are inspired by her world travels on land and at sea. In 2016 she crewed for Gary — a solo sailor who later became her husband. They spent six years cruising the Bahamas and the Caribbean. Her Sunday Times Vikki Orvice Award nominated book, *Flares Up: A Story Bigger Than The Atlantic* (2022), tells the true tale of why two middle-aged men rowed a 20ft wooden boat 3,000 nautical miles across the Atlantic and how the experience affected their families and changed them as human beings.

Her memoir, *Following Sunshine: A Voyage Around the Mind, Around the World, Around the Heart* (2024), the recipient of the International Impact Book Award and the Literary Titan Award for non-fiction and takes readers on a global journey to remote islands and exotic locations, and into the depths of profound love. *A Page From My Life* anthology (2021) features her memoir short *Haul Out,* and her whimsical series *Falmouth Freddy and the Cruising Kanes* appears in Caribbean Compass Magazine. Niamh has also been published in *The Journal, Sail, The Irish Times Abroad, Writing.ie* and *Subsea* magazines. Niamh believes we all have a story to tell and offers writer's workshops in person and online to encourage emerging talent. A lover of dolphins, whales, and all things maritime, Niamh and her husband, Gary, are now based in Southwest Florida.

www.thewriteronthewater.com

Nina Smith

Nina Smith is a writer whose debut novel was selected as a finalist in the Writers League of Texas Manuscript Competition in 2021. She subsequently secured agent representation and enjoyed seeing *What We Don't See,* about a woman who becomes embroiled in the undercurrent of her husband's wrongful arrest, submitted to several publishing houses in North America.

Nina is working on her second novel, another suspense-thriller set in Tokyo, Japan. The corporate setting is loosely inspired by Nina's career in several commercial law firms across the globe (although luckily, no murders have taken place and the characters she works with are infinitely more pleasant).

Nina enjoys reading novels with a strong sense of place, where the location is as much a character as the protagonists, and looks to evoke this in her own writing, which is heavily inspired by her extensive travels. Originally half-British and half-Danish, she has recently settled in Australia with her husband, daughter and dog, following an eight-year stint as an expatriate in Albania, Japan and then the US.

When not writing, Nina works in business development and is the founder of a period underwear company, Fri Period. She also spends a lot of time at the beach.

Instagram: ninasmithwriter

Ben Tufnell

Ben Tufnell is a writer and curator based in London. He has published widely on modern and contemporary art, in particular on artforms that engage with ideas of landscape and nature. His books include *Land Art* (Tate Publishing, 2006), *On The Very Edge Of The Ocean* (Tate St Ives Research Series, 2006), and *In Land: Writings Around Land Art and Its Legacies* (Zero Books, 2019).

His short stories have been published by *Conjunctions*, *Litro*, *Lunate*, Nightjar Press, *Storgy* and *Structo*, amongst others. He has been long- or short-listed for prizes including the BBC National Short Story Award, the Sean O'Faolain Short Story Prize, and the Society of Authors' ALCS Tom-Gallon Trust Award for short fiction.

His debut novel, *The North Shore*, was published by Fleet (Little, Brown) in 2023. The *Times Literary Supplement* described it as a 'queer, oneiric, watery fable in which narrative form and logic are in constant flux'. The novelist and critic Nina Allan wrote that '*The North Shore* is that rare beast, a work of folk horror that holds its own with the classics whilst exhibiting genuine points of difference. This is a timeless book, one that will outlast any fashion...'

www.knappedflint.com

Acknowledgments

As we reflect on this anthology's journey, from concept to publication, we'd like to acknowledge the pivotal role so many people played in bringing this creation into being.

Firstly, we owe our gratitude to Anna Davis, founder and director of the Curtis Brown Creative writing school, UK. Without the work she and her team do — uncovering the creativity in all of us, teaching us the craft of prose, and guiding students on the journey from writer to author — this group would never have met, and this book would not exist.

As Anna mentioned in her remarks, it is difficult to find a publisher who will take on an anthology of short stories much less one from multiple authors, so we would like to extend our sincere gratitude to Regan Rothe and the entire team at Black Rose Writing for believing in this project and bringing our stories to a global audience. To David King and the design team, we are so grateful for the time and effort you have put into creating the wonderful front cover.

To editor, Alice Youell, for your attention to detail during the editing phase; your suggestions were insightful and elevated the work into a cohesive whole. To our friends, mentors, fellow writers and early reviewers your feedback has been greatly appreciated. We'd also like to thank the founders and management of ///what3words for their vision and support of this body of work.

Every writer needs a tribe and we each have special individuals we would like to recognize:

Ben extends his deepest thanks to Laura Black, editor of Fictive Dream, who first published a version of ///*iterative.frantic.recital* (entitled *Bodies*). He is also immensely grateful to Charlotte Seymour for her tireless agenting and to Cecilia Gregory for her unwavering support and guidance.

Billy's journey has been enriched by the validation and messages of support from Mick Herron, Kate Bradley, Holly Seddon, and Marn Davies. He finds inspiration in his muse, Victoria Laurence, whose presence has brought glad times and the motivation to keep on keeping on. Joe, George and Martha make him proud every day.

Cathy acknowledges Anne Freeman for her early review of the anthology. She is thankful for the camaraderie and support of her fellow Word Cave writers, her monthly workshop group, family, and friends. Special appreciation goes to Lisa Salmon for her insightful feedback on ///*cure.brings.tribe* during their time at Varuna.

Conor's gratitude goes out to Kay Garcia for all that he is and Áine for her endless hugs. Nuala's brilliance as a Beta reader and the input from the PPP gang has been invaluable. Erin Hallagan Clare deserves special thanks for reigniting his creative path.

Emile's heartfelt thanks go to her mum, Emmie Reijnders, for instilling in her a love of words. Her kids, Tim, James, Adam, and Matthew, keep her grounded and remind her of what truly matters.

Lily's journey has been shaped by the endless patience and belief of Master Seyit. She is grateful to Niamh and her fellow writers for their continuous inspiration and support. Joann is her rock, and Sach, her everything.

Niamh expresses her deepest gratitude to Gary Krieger for encouraging her to embrace her true calling as The Writer On The Water. She'd like to thank her agent, Brian Langan for his steadfast support. Additionally, she appreciates all the efforts of publicist Jane Reilly, Sarah Fitts, Smith Publicity, as well as the countless TV, radio hosts and podcasters who have helped share her message with the world.

Nina is filled with gratitude for Bruce Smith's limitless love and support, and the many adventures that have inspired her stories. Anja, with her boundless love, curiosity and enthusiasm, has opened Nina's heart in untold ways. Joy, her mum, instilled a love of stories and the written word from an early age, and her fellow writers who have provided endless encouragement. As have a cast of cherished friends and family across the world.

Sandy is endlessly indebted to her lovely parents: Alan, who read the earliest draft of her novel and who sadly never saw her work published, and Lorna who shows her every day that life is one big adventure. And her chosen family, Bill for keeping her fueled emotionally and literally, and her dog Rita for keeping her lap warm as she writes.

And most importantly, to you, our readers, your engagement with our stories propels our passion to continue writing. Thank you for taking the time to immerse yourselves in the worlds we have created and allowing our characters to visit your imagination for a while.

With gratitude,

The Authors

Other Titles by Niamh McAnally

"A truly brave, enriching memoir that will
take you on a global adventure."
–Liam Neeson

FOLLOWING
SUNSHINE

A VOYAGE AROUND THE MIND,
AROUND THE WORLD,
AROUND THE HEART

Bestselling author of
Flares Up: A Story Bigger Than The Atlantic
Niamh McAnally

Note from Niamh McAnally

Word-of-mouth is crucial for any author to succeed. If you enjoyed *Stories of Place*, please leave a review online—anywhere you are able. Even if it's just a sentence or two. It would make all the difference and would be very much appreciated.

Thanks!
Niamh McAnally

We hope you enjoyed reading this title from:

BLACK ROSE
writing™

www.blackrosewriting.com

Subscribe to our mailing list – *The Rosevine* – and receive **FREE** books, daily
deals, and stay current with news about upcoming
releases and our hottest authors.
Scan the QR code below to sign up.

Already a subscriber? Please accept a sincere thank you for being a fan of
Black Rose Writing authors.

View other Black Rose Writing titles at
www.blackrosewriting.com/books and use promo code
PRINT to receive a **20% discount** when purchasing.